A King Production presents…

Baller Bitches
VOLUME 3

A NOVEL

JOY DEJA KING

ISBN 13: 978-1-958834-89-3
ISBN 10: 1-958834-89-0
Cover concept by Joy Deja King

Library of Congress Cataloging-in-Publication Data;
King, Deja Joy
Baller Bitches Volume 3: a series/by Joy Deja King

For complete Library of Congress Copyright info visit;
www.joydejaking.com Twitter: @joydejaking

A King Production
P.O. Box 912, Collierville, TN 38027

A King Production and the above portrayal log are trademarks
of A King Production LLC

Dear Readers:

We've finally come to the end of the *Baller Bitches* series and honestly, I feel so sad. I've grown somewhat attached to the characters Diamond, Kennedy and Blair. All these women have characteristics that I see in my own girlfriends or myself... the virtues and the flaws ☺ With that being said, I hope you all enjoy this final chapter in the series and I truly appreciate you all going on this journey with these ladies and me.

Much Love,

Joy Deja King

Dedication

This Book is Dedicated To My:

Family, Readers and Supporters.
I LOVE you guys so much. Please believe that!!

A KING PRODUCTION

Baller Bitches

VOLUME 3
PARTS 7-10

A NOVEL

JOY DEJA KING

Diamond

"Cameron, how long is this going to last? I feel like a stranger in my own home. We don't even sleep in the same bed anymore. What do I need to do to make this right?"

"Turn back time and make different choices; but that's impossible."

"Well, then don't talk about the impossible. Talk about what I can do because I want this marriage to work."

"Diamond, what do you want me to say? You want me to lie to you and pretend that this marriage is gonna work?"

"Wait, are you saying you want a divorce?"

"I don't know," Cameron admitted somberly.

"I made a mistake. Please, don't throw our marriage away because of a mistake."

"You made more than one mistake; you made several and they seem to keep coming back for you to deal with."

"My work with Renny is done; I 'm out of the drug game."

"What about Rico? What happens when he wakes

up from his coma and tells the police it was you that tried to kill him?"

"That will be dealt with."

"Dealt with how? Are you planning on making sure Rico never wakes up from his coma? Answer me, Diamond!" Cameron shouted.

"You know what he did to me."

"Yeah, and it was fucked up, but there are other ways to deal with people that don't include murder."

"So, what am I supposed to do, take a chance that he'll survive and I've got to do twenty or thirty years for attempted murder? While he's free to walk this earth and raise my daughter, and I rot in jail."

"That won't happen. I won't let it."

"If Rico wakes up from his coma, that's exactly what will happen."

"Diamond, I promise you I won't let that happen, whether we stay married or not; but if you have Rico taken care of on your own, then I'm done with you for good," Cameron said, before grabbing his tote bag for practice and heading out.

I sat down at the dining room table and folded my arms, before resting my head on them. I could've fell asleep right then. Not because I was sleepy, but because I was literally exhausted from the duress my marriage was in. My relationship with Cameron was on the verge of complete annihilation and he had my back against the wall when it came to Rico.

Renny promised he would take care of Rico for me but now I couldn't let that happen. As much as I wanted Rico out of my life for good, if having him completely erased meant ruining even a slight chance of saving my marriage, then I would let it be. With my decision made, I jumped up and headed to the bathroom to take a shower. I needed to go see Renny and shut that shit down, before it was too late.

When I pulled up to Renny's crib, I saw him walking out his front door. "I'm glad I caught you before you left," I said, getting out of my car.

"Last time I checked, my cell phone is still working. Why didn't you call me?"

"This wasn't something I wanted to discuss over the phone."

"Diamond, I thought you were trying to stay as far away from me as possible, after what went down with your husband?"

"I was…I mean I am, but I need to talk to you."

"I have some important business to take care of. Can we discuss this later?"

"What I have to say won't take that long. All I need is a few minutes."

"Okay, so what's up?"

"I don't want you to finish off Rico. Just let him be."

"Why would you want that? He can identify you as his shooter."

"I'll deal with that if it happens."

"I hear you, but it doesn't work like that. The hit has already been made. It's out of my hands at this point."

"Renny, you can't be serious. Just call the guy and cancel it. I'll even still pay him. I just want Rico left alone, my marriage depends on it."

"So, you rather risk going to jail, in order to save a marriage that won't mean anything if you have to spend the rest of your life locked up?"

"Yes. If there's a chance that I can save my marriage, then it's worth the risk. Now, please call off the hit."

"Diamond, I'll see what I can do, but at this point it's highly unlikely I can do a thing. The way I operate, once a hit is put in motion, unless it's halted within the first 48 hours, it's damn near impossible to stop. I have no further communication with the hit man. That's to protect myself, so nothing leads back to me."

"I understand. Just see what you can do."

"I will, but Diamond, you have to let things play out on their own. Sometimes, you can't escape your past. The key is finding someone who can accept it."

"If only it was that simple. Besides Destiny, Cameron is the best thing that has ever happened to me. I can't lose him."

"You might have no choice. I'll be in touch."

My heart sank as I watched Renny walk off. I didn't know how I would make it happen, but I was more determined than ever to save my marriage.

Kennedy

"Tammy, how is the confirmation on the guest list coming? This party for the makeup launch is in less than two weeks and things have to be super tight."

"So far, so good; I'm continuing to follow up with our must-have celebrities, but I think you'll be very happy with the final guest list."

"Good. We don't need any snags with this gig, and Chrissy, can you please answer the phone!" I shouted to the new receptionist, the third one in less than two weeks. I had no idea it would be so difficult to find someone who knew how to answer the phone correctly. At least Chrissy was punctual and had a bubbly personality, so I was determined to keep her on permanently. Even if that meant I had to train her personally.

Business had been booming in recent weeks, so I needed all the help I could get, especially since Diamond was a no-show. I mean, she did show up to the office every day, but mentally she had checked out, which basically made her a no-show. She was completely preoccupied with Cameron and what she could do to get their marriage back on track. My heart did go out to Diamond, but there wasn't enough time in the day to play her marriage counselor and run a new business. So, instead of insisting she do some work, I let her flip through the pages of self-help books, looking for marital tips.

"Yes, Chrissy," I said picking up my desk phone.

"There is a Marcus Powell on the line for you."

"Yes, put the call through. Marcus, hi. How are you?"

"Everything is going great and things should only be getting better. Everyone is looking forward to the movie release and we're actually going to have it in New York."

"Really? Last time we talked, you said it was going to be in L.A."

"We scratched. We're going to have a small screening in L.A. with some film critics and industry execs, but the major red carpet premier will be in your neck of the woods."

"Sounds good to me...very convenient. I will personally make sure that Blair is red carpet ready."

"I know you will, but I'm also hoping you can do something else."

"Sure, what is it?"

"I want to hire your company to do the event."

"Really? Wow! Business is really booming right now, but I'll definitely make room for this. A major movie premier will be an excellent look for us."

"I agree. Of course, this is independent of our monthly retainer. You'll be paid a separate fee for doing this event. So, it's a deal?"

"Of course, I'll send over the proposal and cost, so we can get the ball rolling."

"Perfect. I'll be looking out for it. As always, I look

forward to working with you."

"Ditto. Yes!" I screamed and pumped my fist in the air when I hung up with Marcus.

"What has you so excited?" Tammy questioned, after hanging up with her call.

"We just got hired to do the movie premiere for that new film Blair is co-starring in with Denzel Washington."

"Are you serious? That's incredible!"

"Business is rolling in like crazy."

"Yep. I think it's time for you to hire some more staff."

"Hire more staff, so soon?"

"Good morning, Diamond. I didn't even hear you come in."

"I came through the back. Can you believe there are still paparazzi lurking around? They're taking pleasure in the demise of my marriage."

"They are just doing their job, so don't take it personally. Downfall of celebrity marriages sells papers and magazines."

"I'm not a celebrity."

"Diamond, you're the wife of a celebrity. With that come perks and unfortunately a lot of bullshit. You have to deal with it."

"You know what, let's not even discuss this craziness right now. What's up with this need to hire more staff?"

"Marcus just called me and they're having the movie premiere in New York, and he wants us to do the event."

"Get out! That's huge."

"I know. So, of course we're going to need some additional help. I mean, we have a lot of projects, which is great for business, but that requires more staff."

"Especially since I haven't been much help," Diamond said, tossing her purse down before sitting at her desk. "You've been busting your ass and so have you, Tammy. All the while I've been stuck in my own little, pathetic world."

"It's okay. You're going through a lot right now."

"You've been so understanding and I appreciate it, but no, it's not okay. I need to step it up. Tell me what I need to do. I'm ready to get to work."

"Are you sure?"

"I'm positive."

"Then let's get to work. Tammy, while you're making sure our guest list is tight, Diamond, you can focus on the media. Give her the list of names to call."

"Wow, this is a very long list," Diamond said, when Tammy handed her the papers.

"Yes it is. But luckily, Diamond, you're ready to get to work, so let's do it ladies."

Blair

"Tell me the truth, Skee. Did you spike my drink?"

"I already answered your question and I don't like repeating myself."

"I don't believe you."

"Then don't believe me. But what difference does it make? We've had sex how many times, too many to count. You claim you don't remember this last time we had sex or maybe you don't want to remember. Regardless, I promise not to get offended."

"Get offended? Why the hell would you get offended? You're the one that put something in my drink and had sex with me, without my permission."

"I've never had to take pussy in my life and that includes yours. This interrogation is starting to bore me, Blair. If you have nothing else to ask me, then you can leave." Skee stood up from his chair, walked over to his bar, and poured himself a drink. His calm, cool demeanor almost had me believing that maybe he was telling the truth. Maybe I was wrong and I didn't want to admit to myself that I willingly had sex with him.

"Fine, whatever you say, Skee. I'll just have to take your word for it."

"True, but you also come back to me."

"I'm not coming back to you."

"Yes, you are."

"No, I'm not!" I yelled.

"You think saying it louder is gonna make it true."

"You are so fuckin' smug. You just can't imagine somebody not wanting to be with you. But that's very possible."

"You might be right, but that person isn't you."

"Watch me prove you wrong. Goodbye, Skee."

"Go 'head and leave. Run into the arms of that basketball nigga, but it won't change anything. He'll just hold you over temporarily, but he won't kill the urge you'll have to be with me."

I rushed out of Skee's place, without saying another word. I felt like I couldn't breathe. When I got outside I inhaled deeply, taking in the fresh air. I began walking and headed towards Central Park. When I came upon a bench underneath a large tree, I sat down and closed my eyes. I felt like my life was in complete disarray. I still hadn't started my period and I refused to take the test because honestly, I didn't want to face the truth. It was easier for me to pretend that I was just really late, instead of really pregnant. I had to figure something out, so I decided to call Kirk.

"Hey, stranger. I was beginning to think you were never going to return my phone calls."

"I apologize. I've had so much going on. Been working through some things. I hope I haven't been gone too long and you've moved on."

"You're in luck. I'm a patient man. I've been waiting

on you. How 'bout we do dinner tonight."

"Would love to."

"Cool. Is seven good for you?"

"Yep."

"Then I'll pick you up at seven."

"Great, I'll see you then." When I hung up with Kirk, I breathed a sigh of relief. Things with him were so easy and not complicated, unlike with Skee. *If I am pregnant and decide to keep the baby, please let Kirk be the father* I thought, before heading home.

"Kennedy, I wasn't expecting you to be home."

"I know. Trust me, I'm only home because I left some extremely important paperwork here. I accidentally picked up the wrong folder this morning. But I'm glad you're here, because I have some exciting news to share with you."

"Really, what is it?"

"Marcus called and they are having the movie premiere in New York. Not only that, but our company is putting together the event, which means I will guarantee you're the queen of the ball."

"Look at you getting gig after gig. Leaving Darcy and starting your own company with Diamond is the best decision you ever made."

"True dat. I can't lie, I'm enjoying every minute of it. What about you? First, you have the makeup launch party, then the movie premier. You're going to be a busy girl for the next few weeks. Are you ready?"

"Of course, this is what I've been working towards. Everything is finally coming together in my career."

"What about your personal life."

"I'm getting that together, too. I'm actually having dinner with Kirk tonight."

"What about..." Kennedy glanced at my stomach, without finishing her sentence, letting her eyes ask me the question.

"I haven't taken the test yet. I did confront Skee about spiking my drink and he denied it."

"Do you believe him?"

"I don't know, but at this point does it even matter? If I'm pregnant, there's still a chance he could be the father, although I'm hoping it will turn out to be Kirk's."

"So wait, you do think you're pregnant and if you are you're going to keep it?"

"No...I mean I don't know. All this is just speculation. I'm simply thinking out loud."

"You can always end the speculation and take a test. That way, you'll have your answer."

"Kennedy, I don't want to think about any of that right now. We have two major events coming up and I want to focus on that."

"Whatever you want. Just know I'm here for you and so is Diamond. I'm about to go back to the office. Have fun tonight with Kirk and call me if you need me."

"Will do." When Kennedy left, I immediately made a dash to my closet to find the perfect outfit to wear tonight. Kirk hadn't seen me since we had sex for the first time and I wanted to make an awe-inspiring impression. If I was pregnant, then I was determined to make Kirk the baby daddy. Hopefully I could make him fall so deeply in love with me that he wouldn't even ask for a paternity test. That meant I had to get on my job and I had every intention of doing exactly that, starting now.

Diamond

I woke up, once again to an empty bed, without my husband lying next to me. I would give anything to feel his strong, muscular arms wrapped around my waist. I missed his scent, the warmth of his body, and how it filled up my insides. My mind, body, and soul were screaming out for him, but he wasn't trying to hear none of it.

With Destiny at my mom's and Cameron gone, I was alone in a massive penthouse, ready to sing the blues. I opened all the blinds to let the natural sunlight shine through and give the place some life. My heart wanted me to put on some love music, but I didn't feel like being even more depressed, so instead I blasted some ratchet rap music. The hip-hop beats had me nodding my head while I cooked me some breakfast and to my surprise, it was putting me in a good mood. Before long, I was not only nodding my head to the music but also dancing.

While eating some pancakes, eggs, and bacon I sat in front of my computer and started surfing through the blogs. That had now become a daily ritual, thanks to Kennedy. She stressed to me since now I was in the

PR business, it was my job to stay in the loop on all the latest celebrity news. I damn near spit my food out when I came across the headline post:

Breaking: NBA MVP Cameron Robinson Is Seen Entering A NY High-Rise With An Unidentified Woman, Not His Wife...His Marriage Is Over!

My initial reaction was to throw my plate of food at the computer screen, but I caught myself. I reached for my cell phone and called Cameron but it went straight to voicemail. I kept calling, getting the same results. "Turn on your fuckin' phone!" I belted, ready to break my iPhone in a thousand pieces.

This can't be happening to me. I can't believe Cameron has moved on to another woman already. I'm his wife. We took vows. This can't be the end, I thought to myself as I paced back and forth in the living room. I tried calling Cameron again and got nothing. Right when I was about to try again, I saw Blair calling.

"Hey, this isn't a good time. I'll call you back."

"Diamond, I saw the blogs. I want you to stay calm."

"How the fuck can I stay calm when it's splashed all over the place that my husband is cheating and my marriage is over? How in the hell did my life get so screwed up, so fast?"

"You and Cameron are going through a difficult time right now, but you have to have faith you'll get through it."

"Shut up, Blair! Stop acting like my fuckin' life coach. My husband has checked out of our marriage and there is nothing I can do about it. The last thing I want to hear is your words of encouragement." I abruptly ended my call with Blair, ready to try and track down Cameron again, but then I heard the front door open.

"Hey," Cameron said calmly, before closing the door behind him.

"I've been trying to call you."

"I turned my phone off."

"Is it because you've been laid up wit' that woman you all over the blogs with?"

"That woman is my realtor."

"Let me get this straight. You're admitting to fuckin' your realtor?"

"No, I'm telling you that's who the woman is."

"I get it, she's your realtor, but are you fuckin' her?"

"No."

"Then why were you going into an apartment building with her?"

"Because I'm looking for a place to live and she's showing me some apartments. The stupid media took some fuckin' pictures and created an entire bullshit story from it. My relationship with Ebony is strictly business."

"Last time I checked, you have a place to live. You just gon' casually mention the fact that you're looking for an apartment. So, saying you moving out? You leaving yo' family?"

"We need space."

"You mean you need space. How the fuck do you just bypass your wife and go looking for another crib?"

"I told you I wasn't sure if this marriage was going to work. I've been straight up with you from jump." "So, you want a divorce?"

"I don't know if I want a divorce, I just know I need time away from you to figure this shit out."

"Don't you think leaving is only going to cause a bigger rift between us? We need to be here together so we can make this work."

"What aren't you getting? I don't want to be around you. How can I stay married to a woman I don't even trust?"

"But you can trust me. I made a mistake."

"Even after you confessed to everything, you were still trying to have Rico killed and you probably still are."

"That's not true."

"Whatever. Like you would ever admit the truth."

"You want the truth. The truth is, after our conversation about Rico, I went to Renny and told him to call off the hit. He said it was too late. I begged him to please try because I wanted to do everything I can to save my marriage. I'm trying to do better. I want to be the woman you believed you married."

"You really did that?"

"Yes, I did. Renny asked me was I willing to risk going to jail if Rico came out of his coma, just to try and save a marriage that might be over, and I said yes, if there was even a small chance we could make this work. Cameron, I love you more than you could ever know. Whatever I need to do to make you believe in me again, I'll do it."

"I've been questioning and second guessing everything that's been coming out of your mouth lately, but I can honestly say that, I believe you." Cameron put his hand on the side of my cheek and stroked it. His touch sent shivers though my body. I had longed to feel just a hint of love from him again and this finally felt like a start.

"Baby, it's the truth. If I have to spend the rest of my

life proving that I'm a changed woman, then I will. All I'm asking is that you don't turn your back on me and give me that chance to show you. Will you do that?"

Cameron stood there silently, staring into my eyes. I wasn't sure what his answer would be. I couldn't tell if he was giving me a look of forgiveness and new beginnings, or goodbye.

Kennedy

"This event is tomorrow and we still haven't gotten confirmation on which A-list celebrities will be in attendance. That sucks, Tammy."

"Listen, on the record, they haven't confirmed, but off the record I've spoken to their agents and publicists. The majority of them have confirmed they will be there."

"Really?"

"Yes, really. Kennedy, stop worrying. I mean, I know it's natural for you to worry, but this event is going to be a huge success. Diamond got confirmation on all the media outlets. I also got both the Post and Daily News running stories on it today. Here, look in the papers," Tammy said, handing them both over to me.

"Get out! Great work, Tammy," I said, high-fiving her.

"Girl, you know I got you."

"So, everything else is straight, as far as the décor, food, wait staff, etc.?"

"Handled. I was actually about to head over to the venue now, to make sure the special lights and some other things have been set up properly."

"Yeah, you do that. Also, make sure the stage area where Blair comes out, after they announce she's the new face of the makeup line, is on point."

"That's the main thing I want to check on. The company ordered one of those spotlights that's supposed to look really beautiful. I got the call it arrived, but I want to make sure it's been set up properly."

"Yes, go do that. I'm having some other things delivered there too, so stay until everything arrives. If there is even a minor snag, get me on the phone ASAP. If I don't hear from you, I'll still call you later on, to check the status."

"Got you."

After finishing up my conversation with Tammy, I immediately tried to get Blair on the phone. I had barely seen her for the last couple weeks. During our last conversation, Blair mentioned she was trying to make it work with Kirk. In typical Blair form, she had now practically moved in with him, which meant I had limited access to her.

"Hey, Kennedy. What's going on?" Blair answered the phone in an extra chipper voice.

"Nothing much. You sound very happy. I love that!"

"Things have been going great with Kirk, so I'm feeling really good."

"Excellent. So, are you ready for tomorrow?"

"Yes, I am. I still can't believe they chose me to be the face of their line. It's all thanks to you, Kennedy."

"Listen, I'm just doing my job. I present you the opportunity but you're the one that turns that opportunity into a signed, sealed, delivered deal."

"You still deserve props for always hustling to bring

me those new opportunities. You really work your ass off. I can't wait for Mr. Right to come into your life, so you can slow down and have some fun, too. A little love is good for the soul. Trust me, I know."

"Yes, this coming from the woman who loves the idea of falling in love. You're such a romantic."

"True, but I'll keep trying until I get it right. I have a great feeling about Kirk, though. I think this might last."

I was tempted to ask Blair about her pregnancy scare but she had made it clear last time I brought it up that she didn't want to discuss it. I figured since she hadn't brought it up that it was a false alarm or maybe she had decided to terminate the pregnancy. Either way, I would respect her privacy and wait for her to discuss it with me, if and when she chose to.

"I really do hope that everything works out with you and Kirk. He seems to make you happy and that's all I want for you."

"Thank you, Kennedy."

"But on a business note, I want to make sure you're ready for the event tomorrow. There will be tons of press there, so I need you to be at your best. I'm sure you already met with Vince, and you got your wardrobe and everything together."

"Well..." there was a lingering pause.

"Well what, Blair?"

"I've been kinda playing phone tag with Vince. Kirk had a lot of home games the last couple of weeks, so I've been on dutiful girlfriend duty."

I pulled the phone away from ear for a second and then shook my head in frustration. I refrained myself from cursing Blair the fuck out because I knew it wouldn't do any good. I took a deep breath, staying calm before I spoke.

"Blair, when we hang up, I'm going to call Vince. Where are you right now?"

"At Kirk's place."

"I'm going to have Vince come to you within an hour, so you all can figure out what you're going to wear tomorrow. Have you locked down your makeup person?"

"No, not yet."

"I'll get Toya on the phone, so we can get that done too."

"Kennedy, I'm so sorry. Keeping Kirk happy is a full time job. At first things were so new, and he required a lot of my time. We've somewhat established a routine now, so I'll have more time to focus on me."

"Great," I said, through a fake smile. It was the only way I could keep myself from ripping Blair to pieces. "I'll get everything handled, you just make sure to stay exactly where you're at and don't leave."

"I promise, I won't go anywhere."

"Excellent. I'll also call the car service to make sure they pick you up on time for the event."

"That won't be necessary. Kirk is bringing me."

"Blair, do you know how imperative it is for you to be on time for this event?"

"Yes, and I promise I won't let you down. We will be on time. I really want Kirk there with me and he wants to come, too."

"Don't get me wrong, it would be a good look for you all to arrive together. The press will go crazy, but this isn't just about a photo op, you're actually working this event."

"I know and I'll conduct myself accordingly. Don't worry. Plus, Kirk is nothing like Skee. He'll make sure to get me there on time. Kirk won't have me out partying all night like Skee would."

"Okay. Let me make these phone calls. If anything comes up, I'll call you. If I don't speak to you tonight, I'll definitely be stalking you tomorrow. Bye."

Blair had a way of constantly giving me a migraine, yet I still adored her. She was always one step away from fucking up, but on the flip side, Blair always means well. That's probably why I couldn't help but love her.

"I told you this event would be a huge success. Maybe next time you won't worry so much and you'll listen to me," Tammy smiled.

"You won't get an argument from me. Even Blair showed up on time. I'm thrilled you were right. I was having nightmares about this event being a flop and the company being the joke of the industry. This was our first major gig and you know all eyes were on me to fail, especially the witch of the east, Darcy."

"You proved everyone wrong, especially Darcy. Not only that, you looked great doing it. I'm loving that suit."

"Isn't it fab," I said of the red Isabel Marant red trim detail blazer, with matching skinny trousers that had a contrasting satin waistband. I added some sexy to it by wearing a black lace bustier underneath. "Girl, when I saw it, I had to have it. I knew it would make the perfect statement."

"Hell yeah...bossy."

"Exactly."

As I looked around the opulent venue, with soaring double height ceilings, classical motifs with European influences that screamed elegance, I felt so proud of myself. A year ago, I was Darcy's slave, doing these sorts of events, but she was getting all the credit for my hard work. Now, I was no longer standing in her shadow, I had taken Darcy's spot. I had become so engrossed in tooting my own horn that at first, I didn't hear someone calling my name, until I felt Tammy tapping me on the shoulder.

"Kennedy, turn around," Tammy said.

"What are you doing here? There is no way you were invited," I said, when I saw Darcy standing in front of me.

"Kennedy, is that any way to speak to the woman that taught you everything you know?"

"You know what? I'm not going to let you ruin my night. This evening has been amazing and why not let you be here to see me winning. So, by all means, stay and enjoy yourself. Now excuse me, Tammy, lets go get a drink."

"Kennedy, before you go, I wanted to introduce you to my date."

"I don't give a damn about your..." Before I was able to complete my sentence, my heart dropped.

"This is Nigel," Darcy said, with a wicked grin.

"Kennedy, are you okay?" I heard Tammy ask me as I felt my body getting weak and my mind getting fuzzy. I thought I was seeing a ghost. I reached out to touch Darcy's date, to make sure he was real.

"Sebastian, is that you? You're supposed to be dead," that was the last thing I remembered saying, before passing out.

Blair

"Kennedy, are you okay? Somebody get me some water."
A man I had never seen before was yelling out when I
walked up. He was holding Kennedy in his arms and she
seemed completely out of it.

"What happened?" I asked, bending down to make
sure Kennedy was okay.

"I don't know what happened, she just passed out,"
Tammy stuttered, obviously shaken up. "Here's some
water." Tammy handed it to me and I passed it to the man
that was still holding Kennedy.

After Kennedy took a few sips of water, she seemed
to become much more coherent. "Help me up, please,"
she said softly.

"I think you should stay right here for a little while
longer."

"No, I want to get up," Kennedy insisted.

"Kennedy, I think you should take his advice. You
passed out. We need to take you to the hospital, to make
sure you're okay."

"I'm fine. I'm embarrassed enough as it is. So,
please just help me up." The man wrapped Kennedy's

arm around his shoulder and gently lifted her up. He was being extremely attentive to her, almost like he knew Kennedy intimately, but I had never seen him before. Then I noticed Darcy standing off to the side, watching intensely with a smirk on her face.

The man carried Kennedy over to a chair and sat her down, before giving her some more water. "I think your friend is right, we should take you to the hospital."

"I don't need to go to the hospital."

"Yes, you need to go to the hospital right now, so we can find out why you passed out," I said, sitting down next to Kennedy.

"I don't need to see a doctor; I already know why I passed out."

"Why?" I questioned, totally confused. Kennedy glanced over at the man who had helped her, then put her head down.

"I'm Blair, and you are?" I said extending my hand, wanting to find out what the hell was going on. My gut told me the unidentified man could help.

"I'm Nigel," he said shaking my hand.

"No! You're Sebastian," Kennedy snapped, frowning at the man.

"I don't go by Sebastian, anymore."

"Oh really and why is that?"

"Maybe I should excuse myself, so the two of you can talk."

"You don't have to leave, Blair."

"Are you sure?"

"Positive. It'll be good to have you here, in case I pass out again," Kennedy said sarcastically. "Isn't that right, Sebastian...I'm sorry, I mean Nigel."

"Kennedy, I know this must be overwhelming for

you. I had no idea you would be here. I would've never wanted you to find out this way."

"Find out after all these years I thought you were dead, you were actually alive and well. Your mother told me you died in prison."

"I know," he said putting his dead down.

"You know?"

"Yes, I told her to tell you that. I know..."

"We really need to be going," Darcy said, interrupting Nigel mid-sentence. "I hope you're feeling better, Kennedy."

"Like you care. Who invited you anyway?" I spit, wanting to slap the shit out of Darcy.

"Aren't you being snappy? Where's that little meek girl I met months ago?"

"She's long gone. The new Blair has no problem dragging your boney ass out of this party." Darcy and Kennedy's eyes both widened after what I said, but I meant it.

"You should go ahead and leave. I don't want any problems and Darcy is the definition of a problem for me."

"But we need to talk. I have a lot to explain."

"Oh, now you want to explain yourself, after your secret has been revealed; how considerate of you."

"Just give me a chance to explain. Here, take my number," he said, handing Kennedy a business card. "Please, call me. I really do want us to talk," he said, before walking off.

"Girl, what in the fuckin' soap opera hell happened between you and that guy?"

"Can we talk about it tomorrow? I just want to go home."

"No problem. I'll take you. Are you sure you don't want to stop by the emergency room?"

"I'm positive. The only stop I want to make is to my bed."

"Then, off to bed we go," I said, taking Kennedy's hand and helping her out.

"It sounds like all the drama went down last night after I left," Diamond said, between taking bites of her crab cakes."

"You sure did. It was the craziest shit. I'm still trying to figure out who this mystery man is. Kennedy was calling him Sebastian but he said his name was Nigel. Then he was talking about being in jail, dying and coming back to life."

"Girl, shut up! You so crazy."

"Diamond, I'm not making this up. Kennedy always comes across as the most logical, sane one yet she's giving me real life Young and the Restless drama right now."

"If what you're saying is true, although I'm still side eyeing your version of events; but again, if it's true, this is so unlike Kennedy. She's the most drama-free chick I know. In all the years I've known Kennedy, she's never been on a date, as far as I know. She is the quintessential workaholic."

"Exactly. Hopefully we'll get the 411 on this mystery man soon and what role that conniving Darcy played in it."

"Darcy...she was there, too?"

"Yep. This Nigel guy, or whatever his name is, was her date. That is not a coincidence."

"I thought Kennedy was finally rid of Darcy, once she stopped working for her. I wonder what she's up to."

"Whatever it is, it's nothing good."

"Now you got the wheels in my head turning. Is Kennedy meeting us for lunch to give us the tea?"

"Doesn't look that way," I said, looking down at my watch, to see what time it was. "When I got up this morning she had already left. I called to make sure she was okay and she said she was fine, just handling business. I told her we were meeting for lunch and she said she would try to make it. I guess whatever business she's handling has made her unavailable."

"Damn. I was looking forward to finding out what juicy skeletons Kennedy had in her closet."

"Me too, but be patient, it will all come out. While we wait, you can fill me in on what's going on with you and Cameron. Are you all making progress?"

"Blair, I want to apologize again for being a complete asshole to you. I should've never snapped on you like that."

"Girl, you've already apologized like three times. I understand. Thinking your husband is cheating on you would put any woman in a bad mood. Luckily, it was just a realtor and not some groupie he was creeping with."

"True."

"So how are things going?"

"Things are better. He's agreed not to move out."

"That's a start."

"Yeah, but he's still not back in the bed with me."

"Baby steps. It will happen."

"I really want it to. I miss my husband."

"Cameron may not admit it, but he misses his wife too."

Diamond

"Good morning, I was hoping you would still be here."

"Yeah, I was making some breakfast. I'm sure Destiny will be hungry when she wakes up."

"You're the only one that knows how to make French toast the way she likes. It's her favorite. You need to share your secret."

"No can do. My grandmother gave it to me when I was a kid and I promised her I wouldn't share it with anyone else."

"Cute, but listen, I was hoping you would do something for me."

"What is it?"

"I just got a call from Rico's mother."

"What did she want?"

"She asked me to bring Destiny to the hospital to see Rico. She thinks Rico can feel what's going on around him and having Destiny there will help him get better."

"She might be right or she could be wrong. What do you want to do?"

"Destiny does love her grandmother. If it'll give her some sort of peace having Destiny visit, then I feel I should."

"I think you're doing the right thing. So, what do you need me to do?"

"Under the circumstances, I know I might be asking a lot, but I wanted you to come to the hospital with us. I understand if you say no, but I wanted to ask."

"Yeah, I'll go."

"Really...thank you, so much. I'll go get dressed and then get Destiny ready. Thanks again," I said, kissing Cameron on the cheek before going to the bedroom.

Once I was inside the bedroom, I closed the door and stared in the mirror. I had the widest smile spread across my face. The fact that Cameron was even willing to go to the hospital with us, was a step in the right direction. We hadn't done anything as a family in what seemed like forever. Although going to see Rico in the hospital wasn't exactly my ideal family bonding time, but at least we would all be together. For the first time in weeks I was optimistic that Cameron and I might reconcile.

"Grandma," Destiny smiled, reaching her arms out to Rico's mother, when we saw her outside of his hospital room.

"My beautiful granddaughter. I missed you, so much," she beamed, lifting Destiny up, before hugging her tightly. "Diamond, I'm going to go 'head and take her in Rico's room, if that's okay with you."

"Of course, that's why I brought..."

"What is she doing here?" Lela, Rico's girlfriend barked, cutting me off when she came out of his room and saw me. I hadn't seen Lela since she crashed my wedding and this wasn't the time or place for a showdown.

"Diamond brought the baby to see Rico."

"I know she ain't coming in his room since she's the one that put him here."

"Lela, hush yo' mouth with that foolishness. I told you about that and definitely don't speak that nonsense in front of my granddaughter. Now, excuse me, I'm going to take Destiny to see her daddy."

After Rico's mother and Destiny went into his room, Lela walked up on me like she was about that life. I stood silent for second, trying to keep my composure. I didn't want to show my ass in front of Cameron, especially since he knew that I was the one responsible for Rico's predicament. I also didn't want to cause a scene in front of Destiny.

"You might have Rico's mother and everybody else fooled, but I know the truth. The nerve of you to show up here, when you the one that put him in this hospital. But enjoy your freedom while you can, 'cause once Rico wake up the only place you'll be calling home is a jail cell."

"I understand you're concerned about your boyfriend, but don't speak to my wife like that," Cameron said, standing beside me.

"Oh, I see she got you fooled too. But just like she crossed the father of her child, she gon' cross you, too."

"Shut up! You don't know what the hell you're talking about. Unlike Rico, my husband is a good man and I'll never have a reason to cross him. But then again, I didn't cross Rico either. He's done a lot of dirt, so we don't know which one of his enemies decided to get revenge on him."

"Oh please, you're the one that Rico named as his shooter."

"Everybody knows how much Rico hates me. If he

did name me as his shooter, it's because he'll seize any opportunity to try and ruin my life."

"You got all the answers don't you," Lela smacked, rolling her eyes. "All I can tell you is that your time is about to be up. Rico is getting better and soon he'll be out of his coma. When that happens, it's a wrap for you."

"We've heard enough from you. Come on, Diamond, let's go," Cameron said, taking my hand.

"I'm sorry about that," I said, once we sat down in a waiting area.

"That wasn't your fault. She was out of line."

"Thanks for defending me; especially since you know the truth."

"Diamond, I may not agree with everything you've done, but I understand. Rico put you through a lot. Everyone has their breaking point. I just wish you would've turned to me when things first started going bad. But all that's in the past, we have to focus on what's going on right now."

"If Lela has her way, that would mean me going to jail."

"Listen, I told you I won't let that happen. You're my wife, I'm not letting you go to jail," he said, taking my hand.

"Does that mean you want to make this marriage work?"

"Yes, I do. I've been about our family and us a lot lately. I'm committed to you and Destiny and making our marriage work. At first, I think initially I was in so much shock, that I wasn't sure we would be able to make it. But once I got over that and put everything into perspective, I know I want this to work. We took vows, for better or for worse, and I intend to honor them."

"I don't deserve you, I never have. But you're mine and all I can do is thank God for bringing you in my life."

I leaned in to kiss Cameron but we didn't have any time to relish in our newfound commitment. Chaos ensued around us as we heard commotion coming from outside Rico's room. We ran to see what was going on and saw Rico's mother.

Rico's mother was visibly upset and so was Lela. "What's going on?" I asked, taking Destiny, who was crying.

"I don't know. All of a sudden the monitors were going off. I hear all these noises and Rico's body starts shaking. The nurses and doctor comes running in. I don't know what happened. He was fine one minute then..." she couldn't continue, without breaking down and crying.

Cameron came over and took Destiny, while I tried to console Rico's mother. "It's going to be okay. The doctor will take care of him."

Right when I said that, the doctor came out and walked towards Rico's mother. I saw a couple of nurses come out with a solemn look on their faces. "Mrs. Coleman, we did everything we could, but your son's heart stopped and we couldn't bring him back."

"Nooooooo!" Rico's mother cried out. I held her up, so she didn't fall. I hated what Rico did to me, but seeing his mother like this was breaking my heart.

Kennedy

"I'm glad you came," Sebastian said, opening his hotel room door. "I didn't think you would."

"I wasn't at first, but I couldn't stop myself even if I wanted to. I need to understand why you wanted me to believe you were dead."

"Can I at least offer you something to drink, before we have this conversation?"

"I don't want a drink. All I want is answers."

"Kennedy, the truth is I wanted you to move on with your life. I was supposed to serve a lot of time and I didn't want you wasting the best years of your life, waiting around for me to do my bid."

"I would've waited on you forever."

"I know and that's why I had to make you believe I was dead."

"You were supposed to do twenty years, but you're out."

"My mother was able to get me another lawyer and he got my sentence reduced on a technicality. I got out on time served. By the time that happened, my mother already told you I was dead. The damage was done and I didn't want to disrupt your life."

'That's what you call it, disrupting my life. Showing up at my event when I thought you were dead is disrupting my life."

"I swear, I had no idea when Darcy invited me to come with her, that it was your event. I don't even live in New York. I'm based in L.A. I was shocked when I saw you."

"So, you're dating Darcy?"

"She's doing some PR for a business of mine. We've gone out a few times, but it's nothing serious."

"Why didn't you come back for me? Is it because you blame me for what happened to you?"

"Kennedy, please don't cry," he said, wiping away the tears I could no longer hold back.

"Is that why you changed your name, to make sure I could never find out what really happened to you?"

"After I got out of jail, I wanted to try and erase my past. Start over fresh and part of that meant a new name. I hate that I'm hurting you like this."

I rubbed my hand against the side of Sebastian's face. He was as handsome as ever. His light brown eyes still pulled me like the first day I met him, while I was in college. He was the only man I had ever loved. When I thought he was dead, I decided to dedicate my entire life to building a career and giving up on ever falling in love again.

"I'm glad we were able to talk, but I better get going."

"So soon? I don't want you to go."

"If it wasn't for Darcy bringing you to my party, you would've never come back into my life. Now, you're saying you don't want me to go. You already let me go."

"At the time, in my heart I thought I was doing what was best for you. But seeing you again, it changes things."

"I can't do this with you right now. Everything inside of me wants to run to you and be with you, but I'm not some college girl anymore. You broke my heart and even though you won't admit it, I think you blame me and you wanted me out of your life forever. Just because you run into me by accident and it stirs up these old feelings, it doesn't mean it erases the resentment that pushed you away in the first place."

"I don't resent you, Kennedy, never have. I made that decision, not you, and till this day I don't regret it."

"I wish I could believe you, but I don't. I have to go."

"Wait," Sebastian said, grabbing my arm. "I'm going to be in New York for a couple more weeks. You know where I'm staying. If you change your mind, I'll be here."

I released myself from Sebastian's grasp and ran out. If I had stayed even a second longer, I wouldn't have been able to pull myself away from him. My feelings ran that deep. I was still very much in love with him.

"Why am I not surprised to see you?" Darcy said, when I walked into her office. She was standing there in her red pencil skirt and silk white blouse, trying to appear like a respectable businesswoman. But all the designer clothes in the world couldn't conceal what a witch Darcy was.

"Did you accomplish whatever goal you had by bringing Sebastian to my event?"

"I'm not following you, who is Sebastian?"

"Cut the bullshit, Darcy. You know exactly who Sebastian is."

"Oh, you mean Nigel. You have a problem with my date? He is quite handsome, isn't he? If I play my cards right, he might end up being the one."

"Don't hold your breath. From what he told me, he's not taking you seriously at all."

"Keep telling yourself that. This is the same man that wanted you to believe he was dead. His interest in you clearly isn't that serious."

"Darcy, I'm warning you. If you don't stay away from Sebastian, I will ruin your entire career, or better yet what's left of it."

"Oh please, you're threatening me?"

"No, I'm making you a promise. I have a lot of dirt on you, but I've chosen not to use it. But if you push me, I will."

"I don't take well to threats, so unless you can back it up, I advise you to shut the hell up and get out of my office."

"I know this company you're running is really backed by a man named Renny Renaldo, a notorious drug kingpin. Once this comes out, not only will you be the joke of NYC, I'm sure there are a ton of charges, including money laundering that the Feds will charge you with. So, unless you want to spend a few years in jail, stay away from Sebastian. You've been warned."

"Well, then let me warn you. If you bring down me and Renny, be prepared to bring down your own business partner, Diamond."

"What in the fuck are you talking about?"

"You really don't know. I guess everybody in your life likes to keep secrets from you."

"Stop with the riddles, Darcy, and tell me what the hell you're talking about."

"Your partner, Diamond, works for my partner, Renny. They have a long history of doing business together. Illegal business. She's a drug dealer just like Renny Renaldo. Diamond might have retired from the drug game, now that she's hit the lotto and married Cameron Robinson. But best believe your company was funded on drug money just like mine."

"You are such a pathetic liar."

"Nope, the pathetic one is you. At least I was aware of who I was getting into bed with, but you being in the dark shows how naïve you are. I thought I taught you better. You can't play with the big dogs relying on rookie moves."

"There won't be anything rookie about me, when I bring you all the way down, because that's where you're going. And I'll be there to step right over you."

"Kennedy, I was so glad when you called for us to do dinner. These last few weeks have beyond crazy, Rico dying, then attending the funeral, which I didn't want to do, but of course I had to for Destiny. Cameron went with us. He's been amazing lately. But I needed a break from all the madness. Girl, let's get a drink or should we wait for Blair? Honey, I've just been rambling since I sat down, I haven't even asked how you're doing."

"Blair isn't coming."

"Oh, she must be with Kirk. They seem to be going strong."

"I didn't invite Blair."

"Really, why?"

"Because what I need to discuss with you is private. But then again, Blair might already know. I'm probably the only clueless one in the bunch."

"Kennedy, what is wrong with you? You sound upset."

"I am upset. I just found out my business partner is a drug dealer and our company was started off the money you made from illegal activities."

"I don't know what you're talking about."

"Cut the bullshit, Diamond. Don't insult my intelligence even further by telling me a bold faced lie, while you're sitting in front of me."

Diamond put her head down as if trying to gather her thoughts before saying another word. I didn't want to hear anymore of her lies. I wanted the truth. I believed she owed me that.

"You're right. Everything you said is true except for I'm no longer dealing drugs."

"Why would you, your husband is a multi-millionaire."

"I wanted to change my life and stop selling drugs before I even married Cameron. That's why I wanted us to start this business together. I wanted to be legitimate. I needed to become a woman my daughter could grow up and be proud of. I had no intentions of staying a drug dealer forever. When I saw that you wanted to get out of your fucked up situation with Darcy, I thought this could be a win-win for both of us."

"Why couldn't you have just been honest with me? Not only were we business partners, I thought we were friends."

"We are friends. I consider you to be one of my best friends."

"Then how could you keep something like this from me? I bet Blair knows."

"Yeah, she does. But Blair has known me since I was a little girl. We grew up together. She understands certain things about me that even Cameron probably doesn't. No matter how flawed or fucked up things I do might be, she doesn't judge me."

"So, you're blaming me? Because you think I'm judgmental you didn't tell me the truth?"

"No, I'm not blaming you. This is entirely my fault. The truth is I was ashamed of how I was earning my money and what I was doing and how I was living my life. I didn't want you to know. I didn't want anybody to know. The truth coming out almost destroyed my marriage; now, it looks as if it has destroyed my friendship with you."

"Diamond, that's the furthest thing from the truth. I have no room to judge you or anybody else."

"Please. You're Miss Perfect. In all the years I've known you, you've never done anything wrong."

"Diamond, nobody is perfect, including me. Trust me, I've made my mistakes. You're not the only one with secrets."

"What are you talking about? Does it have anything to do with that guy Blair said was at the event a few weeks ago?"

"It has everything to do with him."

"Tell me what happened. I mean, if you don't mind

sharing."

"I've been keeping this secret for so long, I want to share it with somebody before I go crazy.

"You can tell me, Kennedy."

"I was so in love with Sebastian. I met him when I was a junior in college. I met him at a football game. It was the quintessential good girl meets bad boy and falls in love."

"Did he go to school with you?"

"No, he was a street guy, like you," I laughed. But he had such a huge heart, just like you, too." Diamond smiled. "We had this whirlwind relationship. We fell hard for each other."

"So, what went wrong?"

"Everything. One night I was out with one of my girlfriends and I was wasted. I didn't know how wasted I was at the time. Sebastian and I had broken up and I was trying to blow off steam. Him and one of his friends ended up coming to the club we were at. At first, he didn't know I was there. I saw a few girls coming up to him and although he wasn't doing anything, the liquor got the best of me mixed with a lot of jealousy and I started this huge fight with him. It got ugly."

"Are you serious?"

"Yes. After I caused all this unnecessary havoc, I stormed out and Sebastian chased after me. I was driving off and he managed to get in the passenger side of the car. He was trying to get me to pull over because I was drunk and driving erratic but I..." my voiced cracked, as I relived that night.

"It's okay, Kennedy. Don't cry," Diamond said, rubbing my shoulder.

"I wouldn't listen to him. I was out of control. Before I knew it, I swerved to the other side of the road. I remember seeing a car and hitting it straight on, then I passed out."

"You hit another car?" Diamond asked, as her eyes widened.

"Yes. And when I came to, I was in the passenger side and Sebastian was behind the wheel."

"Huh?"

"Yes, I was so out of it that at first I really didn't remember what happened. But when the police arrived, Sebastian said he was driving the car. We weren't badly injured, so he was arrested at the scene. Later on, we found out that the couple in the other car died and Sebastian was charged with aggravated involuntary manslaughter."

"What!"

"Yes, although he wasn't drunk like me, his alcohol limit was above the legal limit. When I remembered everything, and I realized I was responsible for what happened, I was going to go to the police and confess but Sebastian wouldn't let me. He said that I had one more year in college and he wanted me to graduate and make something of myself. He said he was just a drug dealer and I had much more to contribute to this society than he did. His lawyer told us he would only get about three to five years because he had no criminal record. But on the day of sentencing the judge threw the book at him. They gave Sebastian the max, twenty years. I was sick."

"Omigosh, Kennedy, that's crazy."

"The man that I loved more than anything was going to spend twenty years in jail, for something I did."

"For him to sacrifice his life like that for you, he must've loved you just as much."

"I thought so. After he got locked up, I would go see him every weekend. I wrote him a letter each day. I planned on doing every day of that bid with him. When I was about to graduate, I got a job offer, but it was going to take me away from Sebastian, so I declined it. Then a couple months later, his mother said she needed to see me. When I got to her house she told me Sebastian had been killed in jail. A part of me died that day, too."

"But it was all a lie?"

"Yes. He claimed he had his mother lie because he wanted me to go on with my life and not wait for him. But his new lawyer was able to get him out after serving only a few years. So, my thing is why didn't he reach out and try to find me. If I hadn't ran into him, he would've continued to let me believe he was dead. Sebastian must hate me."

"I don't believe he hates you."

"Then why the lies and why didn't he come back to me?"

"I think he wanted to do what he thought was best for you and then things got complicated. But obviously he loves you."

"Do you think he still loves me?"

"There is no doubt in my mind. You never stop loving a woman you would sacrifice your own life for."

I wanted to believe Diamond was right. I had been working my ass off for the last few years, determined to make something of myself, so that what Sebastian gave up for me wasn't in vain. My heart never stopped belonging to him, but now that I knew he was alive, I was scared.

The pain I felt the first time I lost him, I didn't think I was strong enough to go through that again. But after all he had sacrificed for me; Sebastian was worth taking that chance.

Blair

"Baby, don't forget about the movie premier tonight," I said to Kirk, while he was in shower and I was in the bathroom mirror doing my hair.

"I told you I can't come to the premier, I have a game, but I'll be at the after party."

"We'll see. I'm going to miss not having you on my arm tonight. You're always the best accessory."

"Oh, so now I'm an accessory," we both laughed. "And all this time I was thinking you were my accessory."

"You're going to make me come in that shower and slap you."

"Please, do. I would love to feel inside that warm pussy one more time, before I head to practice."

"Don't tempt me. Seeing all those muscles, especially my favorite muscle, through the glass has me ready to strip down and get wet with you. But I'm already running late and I know Kennedy is about to pull out her hair."

"I understand, baby. Go handle your business. I'll see you tonight."

"You better." I blew Kirk a kiss and went in the bedroom to get my purse and phone. I noticed a missed call from Skee and a text message. I had been doing everything possible to ignore him. I was focused on starting my new life with Kirk and that didn't include Skee.

As I headed out, my phone started ringing and at first I thought it was Skee calling back, but it was Kennedy. "Hey, girlie"

"Blair, you're late. Where are you?"

"I'm getting in the car now, on my way. I'll be there shortly."

"Good, we have a super day."

"I know. Don't kill me, but I still have to get with Vince to find something to wear."

"I knew this would happen, so I already took care of it."

"What do mean, you took care of it?"

"I already picked out a dress for you."

"Kennedy, you know I prefer picking out my own clothes."

"Well, when you do things on time, then you can. But don't worry—I picked you out an amazing dress. You're going to shine like the star you are tonight."

"Are you sure? This is a big night for me. I want the dress to be perfect."

"It is, trust me. After all this time, I thought you would. Just hurry. I'll see you when you get here."

When I hung up with Kennedy, all I could do is smile. Tonight was my first movie premiere. I had finally arrived. I was no longer the struggling waitress without direction. I was now a working actress with a major movie role under my belt. Life was good and only going to get better.

"Am I dreaming? This night has been amazing and this after party is incredible."

"You're right. But the most exciting part is that it is all about you," Kennedy beamed.

"True...true," Diamond chimed in.

"I'm so lucky to have both of you, because you guys are my biggest cheerleaders. But technically, since I'm not the star of the movie, then it's not all about me."

"Blair, it is all about you. At the movie premiere, did you see how everyone in the audience reacted when you died? They absolutely loved your character, even if you weren't in the entire movie."

"Kennedy's right. That was a plum role and you nailed it. I see very big things ahead for you. And I can't wait for us to get started. Let's get our glass of champagne and make a toast to the future," Diamond smiled, waving down one of the waiters walking around with drinks.

"We'll take three of those," Kennedy said, when the waiter came over.

"Actually, I'll have some water or juice." Kennedy and Diamond both eyed me suspiciously at the same time. "I guess now is just as good a time as any."

"You're pregnant," Kennedy said, with dread across her face.

"What happened to congrats?"

"There's no need for this," Kennedy sulked, placing her champagne glass down on a table. "I guess that means you're keeping the baby?"

"Kennedy!" Diamond shook her head. "How can you even ask such a question?"

"I mean, let's be honest here. Blair is about to give up a career that we worked our asses off for her to get and she doesn't even know who her baby daddy is. Is that really something to celebrate?"

"Kennedy, stop!"

"No, she's right. This is definitely not the making of a fairytale, but I can't imagine giving up my baby. Even if I don't know who the father is."

"Are you going to tell Kirk and Skee that they might be the father?"

"No, not yet. I'm just getting around to accepting that I'm going to be a mother. But now that I've made my decision to keep the baby, I'm really thrilled. My life is going great and I think it's only going to get better. But the two of you are the only ones I've shared my news with and I'm going to keep it like that for awhile."

"You're practically living with Kirk. You're not going to be able to hide it much longer. How do you think he's going to react when you tell him there's a possibility that Skee might be the father?"

"I'll handle it. When the time is right, I'll let Kirk know about the baby."

"Well, you know we will be here for you throughout your entire pregnancy and after. We can be your unofficial baby daddies until you figure out who the official one is," Diamond laughed.

"I caught that smirk from you, Kennedy," I smiled, playfully slapping her arm.

"Diamond always has a way of making some serious shit funny. But she's right. We're all partners in this. If you want to have this baby, then we support you one hundred percent. Hell, we can line up some maternity wear modeling gigs for you. And I'm sure your baby will be beautiful. We can have he or she do some modeling, too. The point is, we're going to make it work."

"Kennedy, always the business woman. But that's why you're so great at what you do and another reason why I love you, so much," I said, reaching over to give her a hug.

"I love you, too and congratulations," Kennedy smiled, kissing me on my cheek.

"Awww, let me get in on the hug, too. I love you girls, so much," Diamond added.

"If it isn't the woman of the hour," I heard a familiar voice say, before turning around to see his face.

"Marcus, thank you," I blushed.

"I tried to tell Blair it was all about her tonight," Kennedy winked.

"I knew you were the woman for the role and I'm so glad you proved me right. I have big plans for you," Marcus said. "Oh, and by the way, that dress you're wearing, had you looking like the star of the red carpet at the movie premiere tonight," Marcus added before walking off to talk to the movie director.

"Didn't I say you would shine like the star you are in that dress I picked out," Kennedy stressed.

"Yes, Kennedy, you were right."

"And..."

"And, I apologize for ever doubting that you would pick out the perfect dress for me to wear tonight." Kennedy really did outdo herself with the dress selection. The Donna Karan Atelier design featured sparkly silver bugle bead embroidery, a draped neckline and a tulle train. All I had to do was add a clutch and a bold red lip as my accessories.

"You two are so silly," Diamond chuckled, shaking her head at Kennedy and me.

"Speaking of silly, or better yet, a clown, guess who's walking towards us?"

Before I could even guess who Kennedy was talking about, Skee was standing in front of me. Before Skee had a chance to open his mouth I started feeling nauseated. I wasn't sure if it was due to my pregnancy or seeing Skee's face.

"I apologize for not making it to the movie premiere, but I wanted to make sure I came to the after party."

"I had no idea you were invited," Kennedy mocked, while dangling her glass of champagne in her hand.

Skee shot a cold stare in Kennedy's direction, before saying in his typical narcissistic tone, "I'm invited to everything."

"Skee, you really didn't have to come."

"I wanted to. I also wanted to give you this," he said, pulling out a small jewelry box. "Since you rarely take my calls these days, I didn't know when I would have another chance to give you this gift."

"I can't take a gift from you."

"Yes, you can and you will," Skee said, trying to put the small box in my hand.

"No, I can't," I said, pushing it away.

"We need to talk."

"Yeah we do, but not here, not now."

"Yes, here and yes, now. Let's go outside," he said, eyeing the open doors that led to the terrace outside. Skee put his hand around my arm, gripping it firmly. I didn't want to make a scene so I kept my cool and obliged his demand.

"Ladies, I'll be right back. I'm going on the balcony

to speak with Skee for a moment."

"We'll be here if you need us," Diamond smiled.

"You can take you hand off of me, Skee. I'm going outside to talk to you. No need for the manhandling."

Of course, Skee ignored me and pushed through the crowd of partygoers, until we reached the terrace. Once we got outside, Skee took it upon himself to close the double glass doors, as if this was his home and he could do whatever he like.

"Why do you have to make things so difficult?"

"Difficult? Because I don't want to take your gift, I'm being difficult?"

"Yeah, I would say so. Tonight was a big deal for you. All I'm tryna do is show my support and you shut me down. That's unnecessary."

"I just don't want you to get the wrong idea."

"Which would be?"

"If I accept your gift, you might think that means I'm accepting you back in my life."

"Is that what you really want, Blair, me out of your life? I have no desire to pursue a woman that doesn't want me. If that's what you truly want, then I'll walk through those doors and I'll never bother you again. That's a promise."

I could hear the seriousness in Skee's voice. I didn't know if it was because he might be the father of my unborn child or if I wasn't ready to shake this unhealthy attachment I had for him but I felt my heart beating rapidly. A fear shot through me. I leaned back on the balcony almost losing my balance. Skee reached out, taking my hand so I didn't fall.

"Are you okay?"

"Yeah, I didn't realize how low the banister was.

I'm fine, thank you. But to answer your question, I'm not saying that."

"Of course you're not, because you know there's a connection between us. You don't want me out of your life, no more than I want to be out of it. Now, open this," Skee said, handing the jewelry box to me.

"They're beautiful," I said, of the Lorraine Schwartz canary yellow diamond earrings.

"When I saw them, I knew I had to get them for you."

"Buying me diamond earrings doesn't change all the bad things in our relationship."

"I know that. But I'm a work in progress, Blair. What's normal to you and other people is not what my world consists of. But I want you in my life, so I'm tryna make some adjustments. It's gonna take some time though. It's not gonna...."

"So, this is where you are. I've been looking for you." Skee and I both turned to see Kirk standing in front of the now opened glass doors.

"Kirk, hi. I'm so glad you made it."

"Of course. I told you I would."

"So, you invited yo' lil' basketball friend, but you didn't invite me?"

"Skee, don't do this," I huffed.

"Yeah, she did. That means Blair wanted me here, so now you can be gone."

"I ain't going nowhere. As a matter of fact, you need to leave 'cause we having a private conversation that you interrupted," Skee said, walking up on Kirk.

"When you gon' realize your relationship with Blair is over? She wit' me now. I'm her man."

"You really ain't nothin' but a dumb jock, if you believe that shit. Blair, will always come back to me, you pussy ass nigga."

"Nigga, you the pussy," Kirk shot back, before swinging on Skee.

"That's enough! The two of you stop!" I screamed out, but it didn't matter because within a matter of seconds, all I saw were fists swinging. Kirk and Skee were throwing blows and as the brawl headed in my direction, I tried to move out of the way, but it was too late. Their powerful bodies pushed up against mine, jolting me up in the air, and falling backwards over the balcony.

"Help me!" I screamed out, as I tried to hold on to the banister. My hands were getting weak and I felt them about to slip. Kirk and Skee were so engrossed in their fight, it wasn't until I screamed out a second time that they realized what had happened.

"Take my hand," Kirk said in a panic.

"And I'll take your other and we'll lift you up." Both men were reaching out their hands but I was afraid to let go of the banister thinking I would fall.

"Omigoodness, Blair!" Kennedy and Diamond screamed, when they looked over the balcony and saw me. A crowd had now gathered and as my reality sunk in, tears began streaming down my face.

"You have to help her and she's pregnant," Diamond blurted out

"Pregnant?" both Kirk and Skee said in unison.

Saving my life and my unborn child's was the only thing I could think of at the moment, so I wasn't in the state of mind to respond. All I was trying to do was hold on and survive.

"Please, don't let me fall," I begged, as I looked into both Kirk's and Skee's eyes.

Diamond

"No! She's slipping away," I cried, covering my mouth. "Skee, don't let her go," I screamed out. Kirk seemed to have a better grasp of Blair's hand, but because the way her body was turned, Skee wasn't able to get a firm grip.

My heart was racing and I knew Kennedy's was too but she held my arm trying to calm me down. We could see the tears flowing down Blair's face as her legs dangled. When one of her stilettos slid off her foot and hit the pavement, we all let out a loud gasp. Thinking for a second Blair was on her way down, about to hit the ground too.

"Skee, I'm 'bout to lean down over the banister and try to pull Blair's body over. But I'ma need you to hold on to her arm as tightly as you can. Okay?"

"Got you," Skee said, nodding his head.

"Kirk, that seems risky. What if you're not able to get a good grasp on Blair and instead of pulling her up, your weight makes you both fall over?" I questioned.

"Diamond, it is risky, but we're losing our grip on her. I don't know how much longer Blair can hold on. We're running out of options, but I think this will work.

When I say pull, just pull, Skee."

"I'm ready," Skee insisted as sweat trickled down his forehead.

"Blair, I'm leaning over to pull you up by your lower body. I have to let go of your arm for a second, but Skee is going to hold you up by your other arm. Don't panic... are you with me?"

I could see Blair locking eyes with Kirk and her fear was undeniable. She didn't seem confident in his plan, but was willing to put her trust in him. "Yes," she responded, with her voice trembling.

I was praying Kirk's athletic NBA body was worth all the millions he was being paid and could somehow pull off a miracle, but in my heart, I wasn't so sure. Kennedy and I held hands tightly as we watched in horror as Kirk slowly maneuvered his body over the banister, still holding on to Blair's hand.

"I'm about to let go," Kirk told Blair. "When I do, I want you to try as hard as you can to lift your body towards me. Skee will also be pulling your body towards us too. You can do this, okay," he said, in the most encouraging tone Kirk could muster up under the circumstances. "Are you ready?"

"Yes, I'm ready," Blair said.

"What about you, Skee... are you ready?"

"Got you man, I'm ready."

"1... 2... 3... go!" I heard Kirk say before I closed my eyes shut, unable to watch the rescue mission unfold. I wasn't a smoker but my nerves were so bad, I needed a pack of Newport and a bottle of hard liquor. Right when I gathered enough courage to open my eyes, I heard a loud piercing scream. I quickly turned my head away, believing Blair had fallen to her death.

Kennedy

"Thank goodness she's alive... she's alive!" I yelled out, rushing over to Blair.

"Girl, I almost had a heart attack because of you." Diamond wept, kneeling down next to Blair.

"I'm sorry. I seem to get myself in one messed up situation after another," Blair said, letting out a deep sigh. "Do you think my baby's okay?" she asked, putting her hand over her stomach.

"We need to get her to the hospital," Skee said, not letting go of Blair's other hand. "Did the ambulance get here yet? If not we'll have my driver take her."

"That won't be necessary, my driver can take her," Kirk interjected.

"My driver is parked right in front," Skee said.

"So is mine," Kirk shot back.

"Can we not do this right now. Both of you need to set your ego aside and..." before I could finish my thought I noticed the paramedics arriving and a sense of relief came over me. The last thing I wanted to do was argue with two grown men. My only concern was making sure Blair and the baby were fine.

"Do you think the baby is okay?" Diamond questioned as she fidgeted with her iPhone. "Why isn't Cameron answering his phone or responding to my text messages?" she then asked, looking at me with a frazzled expression on her face, knowing I didn't have the answer.

"Diamond, breath and try to relax. Getting yourself worked up isn't going to make things better. We just have to wait and see what the doctor says."

"Kennedy, how can you remain so calm? It amazes me how you're able to stay cool under any circumstances."

"Trust me that's not the case. I have been on the verge of a major nervous breakdown on more occasions than I care to remember, but through those experiences, I've learned that under the worse of circumstances keeping your cool is imperative. Especially when everyone around you is falling apart."

"I guess I am being a tad overly dramatic." Diamond laughed nervously.

"Actually I wasn't talking about you. I was referring to Skee and Kirk. If the paramedics hadn't showed up when they did, the two of them would have went to blows over whose car was going to take Blair to the hospital. They can't even put their egos aside for the well being of Blair's unborn child. I'm used to that sort of narcissistic behavior from Skee, but I expected better from Kirk."

"I feel you but to be fair both men did just find out Blair is pregnant. I'm sure they're both side eyeing each other wondering if the other is the father."

"True, but they could show a little restraint. I mean Blair did almost fall over a balcony and die due to a fight they started," I said in disgust. "It's time for both of them to grow up, especially since one is about to be a father."

"You won't get an argument from me about that," Diamond said, before focusing her attention on her phone. "This is Cameron. Hold on for a sec," she said, before answering. "Babe, where have you been?"

"Sorry I had fallen asleep. I woke up a minute ago and saw I had missed your calls and your text messages," I heard Cameron say, since Diamond was standing right next to me.

"Sleep?" she asked with a frown on her face.

"Yeah. So how is Blair, is she okay?"

"Yes, she's fine, we're just waiting to hear if the baby is okay. Are you coming to the hospital?"

"I don't think that's a good idea."

"Why not?"

"You already said both Skee and Kirk are there. We don't want to turn the hospital into a circus. The media will get wind of this soon, if not already. I don't want my presence to add to the commotion. Just keep me updated. I'll be here when you get home."

"Okay, I love you," Diamond said, with disappointment in her voice.

"Love you, too."

"Something is up with Cameron," were the first words out of Diamond's mouth when she hung up with her husband.

"Why do you say that?"

"I have never known Cameron to fall asleep this early."

"Girl, chill. Don't start getting paranoid."

"I'm telling you, Kennedy, something ain't right with

my husband, but I can't think about that right now. I'll get to the bottom of that shit after we see what's up with Blair's dilemma," Diamond reasoned.

Although Diamond was trying to keep her composure, her body language was giving me nothing but panic. Her and Cameron had been through so much the last few months, so I had my fingers crossed that her suspicions were off base. They hadn't had any real peacefulness since walking down the aisle. There had been one set back after the other and I thought they had finally got it together. Between Blair's love triangle, me finding and seeming to lose my lost love and Diamond's marriage woes, none of us seem to be winning in the game of love.

Blair

"Is the baby mine?" were the words that greeted me when the doctor exited the room and left me alone with Skee and Kirk.

"Kirk, do we have to discuss this right now?" I asked, before anxiously glancing over at Skee. I had no clue if he was about to spill our sexual encounter from a few months ago. This was definitely not the time, given the fact I was practically living with Kirk.

"Is the baby mine or not, Blair?" Kirk continued to press, not backing down from his question. The anger in his voice was making my head throb.

"Maybe you need to take it easy, Kirk. You heard what the doctor said. She doesn't need any additional stress. Blair almost died because of us," Skee stated, before turning towards me and saying, "and I'm sorry about that, Blair. I had no idea you were pregnant but that still doesn't excuse my behavior."

"How would you know she's pregnant, she's my woman not yours," Kirk spit, as his jaw flinched.

Before another verbal lashing jumped off between

the two of them, I shut it down. "Listen, I'm not feeling good and I don't want to get upset because it might trigger unnecessary stress to the baby. The doctor said they want to keep me here overnight to monitor the baby, so can you both go so I can get some rest."

"I understand. When you get released tomorrow I can hire a nurse to stay with you so you can have 24-hour care. I don't want you worrying about anything," Skee said.

"Blair doesn't need you doing shit for her. I'll be here to pick her up from the hospital and she's coming home with me. Whatever she needs, I'll provide it," Kirk made clear.

"Excuse me, you have two women here to see you," the nurse said, entering the room. I welcomed her interruption because I was ready for both Skee and Kirk to leave. "Would you like to see them?"

"Yes, please send them in," I said, figuring it was Kennedy and Diamond.

"Blair, I'll be here in the morning to pick you up," Kirk said, before walking out.

"Okay. I'll see you then."

"Call me if you need anything," Skee said, before heading out.

"She won't be needing anything from you," Kirk shot back, as Diamond and Kennedy entered the room.

"I can't tell you how happy I am to see the two of you." I exhaled, once the room was cleared out with only my two best friends left inside.

"Girl, I can only imagine the foolishness that was taking place with those two clowns in the same room," Kennedy chuckled, as she came over and gave me a hug.

"You had us so worried! How's the baby?" Diamond asked, after giving me her own hug.

"The baby is fine, thank goodness."

"God is good. I can finally relax," Diamond sighed in relief.

"Yes He is. You all, I literally saw my life flash by as I dangled from that balcony, holding on for dear life. At that moment, I truly understood how precious life is and the life of my unborn child," I admitted, patting my stomach.

"I can only imagine what going through a traumatic experience like that will do to you," Kennedy said, nodding her head.

"Based on the conversation that took place in this room, the drama has only begun."

"What do you mean, Blair?" Diamond inquired.

"Kirk asked me point blank was the baby his." Both Kennedy's and Diamond's eyes widened in dismay.

"What!" they said in unison.

"Yes. He was determined to get the answer too until Skee was the voice of reason to let it go for now."

"I never thought I would hear voice of reason and Skee in the same sentence," Kennedy hissed.

"Yes, I was surprised too. I'm dreading seeing Kirk tomorrow. I wasn't ready to come clean with him, but now I don't have a choice. He's not going to take the news good." I sighed as my eyes watered up.

"Blair, don't cry," Diamond said, stroking my hair. Kirk might've been a little aggressive tonight, but after he sleeps on it and calms down he might be a lot more understanding than you think."

"Diamond's right. Give Kirk a chance to cool down. He cares about you a lot. It's understandable for him to be turnt up right now, but he'll pull it together," Kennedy insisted.

"I hope you're both right. I was hoping for a peaceful pregnancy, but that might be wishful thinking."

"You will have a peaceful pregnancy. The health of your baby is the most important thing. If Skee and Kirk don't understand that then you'll have to cut them off until the baby is born. I know that isn't an ideal situation but your priorities are different now. You're going to be a mother," Kennedy said.

"You're absolutely right. I have to be honest with Kirk and deal with the ramifications. If that means losing him then so be it. I didn't want to go through this pregnancy alone, but I might not have a choice."

"Blair, you won't be alone. Before all the craziness broke out tonight, we told you that we would be your unofficial baby daddies until further notice. That hasn't changed, has it, Kennedy?"

"Nope. Diamond and I are more than capable of fulfilling the role of your baby father until you find out who the actual daddy is."

"I'm so lucky to have both of you. You're making what could be a complete nightmare into something beautiful."

"You're carrying a life inside of you, of course it's beautiful. I remember when I was pregnant with Destiny. Through all the hell Rico put me through during my pregnancy, feeling my baby growing inside of me made it worthwhile. Blair, you're truly blessed. I would give anything to be carrying Cameron's baby right now."

"Diamond, you will," I said, realizing for the first time how badly she wanted to have a baby with Cameron.

I knew they planned on having a child together but there was a sound of desperation in Diamond's voice that had me concerned.

"Give yourself some time. You and Cameron will give Destiny a little brother or sister before you know it," Kennedy said, trying to reassure Diamond.

"Knowing Blair is with child is making me overly sentimental. I'm fine," Diamond smiled but I knew she was lying. We had been best friends for most of our lives and I knew her almost as well as I knew myself. I wasn't sure what was going on in her marriage, but I hoped whatever it was, they would work it out. I needed Diamond to be strong more than ever right now because my personal life was headed to shambles.

Diamond

"Good morning, baby," I said, sneaking up behind Cameron and wrapping my arms around his waist. "I thought I would wake up with your warm body by my side, especially since you were sleep when I got home last night."

"I got up early and worked out," he said, quickly kissing me on the forehead before hurrying out the kitchen.

"Why are you in such a rush?" I asked, following behind him.

"I don't wanna be late for practice."

"Practice doesn't start for another couple of hours," I said glancing over at the clock.

"I know but I have a few stops to make before then."

"Cameron, what is going on with you?"

"What are you talkin' about?" he turned and said with one hand on the doorknob.

"First, you're going to sleep early as hell, then you bolt out the kitchen like you don't want me touching you. Are you mad at me... did I do something wrong?"

"Baby, no. I'm sorry. I have a lot on my mind. We're

trying to make the playoffs and my game is off. It's putting me in a bad mood."

"I'm sorry, babe. Don't put so much pressure on yourself. You'll work it out," I said, walking over and giving him a kiss.

"Why don't we get dressed up and go out to dinner tonight. We'll go to your favorite restaurant. The one that is ridiculously overpriced, but you love the ambiance, as you like to put it," Cameron smiled.

"For real, we can go there tonight?" I grinned.

"Yes. I'll call and make reservations."

"You're Cameron Robinson, you don't need to make reservations." I laughed, leaning up and nuzzling the tip of his nose.

"You're so cute. I'll see you later on."

"Okay, I love you."

"I love you too, baby."

I was beaming after Cameron left. I had my husband back. I knew something was off with him but now it all made sense. With all the perks of being an NBA wife, one of the downsides was that their moods were so linked to how they were playing the game. If the team was winning and they were making the big shots, all was good in life. But if they were losing and coming up short then everybody had to suffer, and the brunt of that fell on the wife. Based on conversations I had with some of the other girlfriends and wives of guys in the league I had already prepared myself for it. It came with the territory. I was just thankful that I knew what was wrong with my husband and could stop driving myself crazy trying to figure it out.

I decided I wanted to wear something special for my night out with Cameron, so I hit up all the high-end boutiques on Fifth Avenue. I could've easily done major credit card damage, but I quickly found the perfect raspberry halter dress with gold hardware accents in the Gucci store. All I needed now was the right shoes, which I found at Fendi. They were mirrored leather sandals in shades of champagne, blue, and raspberry with a white lacquered double heel. The shoes almost seemed custom made to match my dress. I left the store with bags in tow, smiling from ear to ear. I imagined the lust I would see in Cameron's eyes when I stepped out on his arm looking liking the sweetest piece of candy. Having visions of my husband slipping the dress off my body once we got home after dinner, made me oblivious to everything and everyone around me. My head was so far up in the clouds that it wasn't until I felt someone grab my arm that I snapped out of my daydreaming.

"You didn't hear me calling your name," Lela popped, still holding my arm.

"Who the fuck are you talkin' to and get yo' motherfuckin' hand off of me," I belted, yanking my arm loose.

"Look at you. Strolling down this little ritzy street, spending your husband's money like you ain't got a care in the world. All while Rico is dead and buried 'cause of yo' trife ass."

"Are you following me because Fifth Avenue is a far cry from the animal shelter you call home. They decided to let you out your cage so you could go for a walk?"

"Make jokes all you want, Diamond, but you going down. Not even all your husband's millions is gonna keep you out of the six by eight foot cell you'll be spending the rest of your life in. So the only person that's going to be in a cage is you."

"Lela, stay the fuck away from me or you'll be the one facing criminal charges for harassment and stalking. You need to get yo' life. Rico is no longer here. It's time for you to move on. Wasting your time tracking my moves isn't gonna bring him back."

"Following you isn't a waste of my time at all. I want you to see the face of the person who is gonna bring you down for killing Rico."

"Like I told you before, I didn't kill Rico. If you had any proof showing otherwise you would've been gone to the police, instead being up in my face."

"You think you got it all figured out," Lela smirked, "but you don't. Enjoy your freedom while you can because it ain't gon' last."

I wanted to wrap Lela's ponytail around my fist and drag her ass up and down 56th Street. I wasn't sure what pissed me off more. The fact that this scallywag was trailing me like she was some low budget private detective or that she wouldn't let this Rico situation go. I thought by now she would've given up on her quest to prove I was the one that killed her man and be laying on her back under the next doughboy. But no, Lela seemed more determined than ever to show I was the one responsible. It was becoming a tad bit scary. It's like she adopted the hard on for me that Rico left behind after he died.

"Lela, I understand you grieving so I'ma try to excuse your borderline psychotic behavior. But I'm only giving you this one last pass. You showed out at the hospital, now you're showing out in the middle of the street on this beautiful afternoon. You have completely worn out the little patience I had left for you. So take my advice and get over this fixation you have of bringing me down. Because if you really believe I killed Rico, just imagine what I can make happen to you. Now step," I warned, never breaking away from my icy glare.

Lela continued to stand in front of me for a few seconds with her arms folded like she was ready to go to war. But after I dropped my bags and balled my fist like, "you wanna go to war, fuck it we can go to war," she backed down and walked away. Did I really want to fight this chick in the middle of the day with a ton of witnesses, hell no but I couldn't let her know that. Lela had the potential to be dangerous because she didn't seem to have anything to lose. But one thing I had learned from when I hustled in these streets, everybody had a weakness. I had to figure out what Lela's was so she could leave me the fuck alone.

Kennedy

"Kennedy, I think you should take a look at this," Tammy said, as soon as I walked into the office.

"Damn, can I at least sit down first." I laughed, tossing my purse on my desk. Tammy walked over to me with her laptop in hand, ignoring my request. "Wow, this must be awfully important," I commented, not even getting a half grin from Tammy.

"Read this blind item," she said, pointing to a story on a major blog that we frequently fed stories to for some of our celebrity clients. I read the item with rapid speed, and did so a few more times to soak it all in.

What superstar NBA player might have already traded his Diamond in for gold? Word on the curb is that he is the latest celebrity to have one of those so called "on a break" babies on the way. The only difference is, he doesn't have a girlfriend or fiancé but a wife. Who do you think it could be? Leave your comments below.

"This blind item sounds a lot like Cameron and Diamond, don't you think?" Tammy said, shaking her head.

"It can't be," I said, refusing to believe that this was about Cameron. "This is some disgruntled groupie trying to start trouble," I huffed, pushing Tammy's laptop away.

Tammy shot me a, "bitch please" look but I pretended not to notice. This was the sort of drama that I wanted no part of. If I let myself believe there was remotely any truth to it, I would feel obligated to tell Diamond. I didn't want to be the one to bring this bullshit to her. My initial reaction was to call Blair and ask her what she thought about it. Then I remembered she was still in the hospital because the doctor had her stay for a few more days, due to some cramping in her stomach. The last thing she needed was any additional stress.

"So are you going to show Diamond this?" Tammy asked, interrupting my deep thoughts.

"No and don't you say anything to her either."

"Okay, but she's going to hear about it eventually once all the other blogs pick it up."

"Hopefully nobody else will pick it up. It's a blind item for heaven's sake. Most of the reputable blogs are going to want to see some receipts. Clearly whoever leaked this story doesn't want to show any."

"Maybe or maybe this is a teaser before the real tea is spilled. You know this blog is good for getting exclusives... I mean we've given them a few."

"Tammy, shut up. This is hitting way too close to home. I need to figure this out or better yet find out if it's true or not. I'm trying to think who we can call that would be willing to talk."

"Nobody. If chess moves are being made behind the scenes then no one is going to show their hand until the time is right."

Tammy was working my very last nerve with all her

industry talk but I knew she was right and it was pissing me off. If this tragedy didn't involve Diamond I would simply brush it off as just another juicy story, but it was so much more than that. As my head was spinning out of control, I noticed a text come through from Sebastian. He wanted me to come to his hotel so we could talk.

"Tammy, I have to step out for a minute. Hold things down until I get back. Remember, if Diamond shows up before I get back don't you say a word to her."

"What if she brings it up to me."

"She won't."

"What if she does?"

"Pretend that you don't know what the hell she's talking about. This is a very delicate situation. Hopefully this will be the last we hear about it and it will magically disappear. If not, then I need to see if this shit is fact or fiction before Diamond finds out."

"Yes boss, I will follow your orders. But I suggest you get to digging quickly, because I have a strange feeling this rumor has only begun and will be spinning out of control."

"Then stop standing here running your mouth to me and start talking to some of your sources. I need answers and I don't care where they come from," I said, before grabbing my purse and heading out.

When I knocked on the door of Sebastian's hotel room, my nervous excitement diminished rapidly when I saw Darcy sitting down on the couch after I walked in. She had her long bony legs crossed, sitting upright with that uppity smirk on her face that I detested.

"Kennedy, thank you so much for coming," Sebastian said, taking my hand.

"What is she doing here?" I asked, frowning at Darcy.

"She just stopped by to drop off some papers. I didn't know she was coming when I invited you over. But we're done here and Darcy was about to leave."

"Yes, I am. Nigel, call me after you've had a chance to go over everything and let me know if it's to your liking." She smiled.

"His name is Sebastian," I hissed.

"Oh really? On the last check I cashed from him, it said Nigel."

"Didn't I tell you to stay away from him?"

"Calm down, Kennedy. No need to have a hissy fit. I know you're dealing with a lot right now. I don't want to add anymore strain," Darcy said, with a devilish grin.

"You don't know what I'm dealing with, so save it."

"I apologize, I just assumed you would be dealing with that unfortunate scandal that's brewing. I'm surprised you're not somewhere consoling your business partner. I'm sure she needs all the support she can get right now."

"What in the hell are you talking about, Darcy!"

"Kennedy, you're in the PR business. It's imperative that we stay on top on all of the latest gossip. So I'm sure you've already heard about Cameron," Darcy remarked.

"You mean that ridiculous rumor that some bitter trick is spreading."

"Be careful, Kennedy. I would never leak a story unless I had verified it."

"You were the one that gave the blind item to the blog?" Kennedy asked bewildered.

"I can't take full credit, the information practically

landed in my lap. All I had to do was make a phone call."

"How dare you start such a vicious rumor!"

"Baby girl, I see you still like to keep your head in the clouds. This isn't a rumor, it's fact. Your friend's husband has a baby on the way. The full story will be breaking soon so I suggest you prepare Diamond for the fast approaching storm."

"You lowlife heffa," I barked, lunging at Darcy.

"Kennedy, calm down," Sebastian said, holding me back. "Darcy, it's time for you to go. I'll be in touch."

"I look forward to it. Enjoy the rest of your day, Kennedy," she said before making her exit.

"How do you deal with that woman... she is poison!" I screamed, tossing my purse down.

"Darcy has her issues but she's good at what she does. It's business for me. She's been delivering and that's the bottom line. But I didn't ask you over here to discuss Darcy."

"What do you want to discuss?"

"Us. Or at least if there is a possibility of an us."

"If I'm answering with my heart then the answer is yes but—"

"But nothing. All I care about right now is what is in your heart. Everything else can be handled."

After all this time, Sebastian was still the same confident and fearless man that I remembered from years ago. Just like when he was sentenced to all those years in prison. His mother and I broke down and cried our hearts out as we held each other in the middle of the courtroom when the judge made the ruling, but not Sebastian. He kept his head up, smiled at us and said he would be fine and he was right.

"Life isn't black and white, Sebastian."

"In most cases it could be, but you rather look at things as being gray because nothing makes sense to you unless it's complicated."

"That's not true."

"Are you sure?"

"Yes," I said adamantly.

"Then prove me wrong," Sebastian said, now standing directly in front of me. He leaned in and pressed his soft lips against mine before I could even say a word. I closed my eyes and found myself going limp in his arms. The sparks that shot through me in the past from Sebastian's touch, were still in full affect. Nothing had changed only time.

I wasn't sure if it was because I hadn't felt a man's touch in what seemed like forever, or that I missed and still loved Sebastian, or if he was just fine as hell and was totally turning me on. But in a matter of a few short minutes, I went from kissing Sebastian in the sitting area of his hotel suite to being completely naked laid across his king-sized bed. My body began to shiver as he gently sprinkled kisses from my neck all the way down to the back of my legs, not missing a spot. Sebastian took his time, as if he knew he was awakening the naughty girl in me that had been asleep for way too long. As I moaned in pleasure my eyes widened in lust at the sight of Sebastian's damn near perfect crafted frame after he took off his shirt and jeans. I remembered him having a nice body, but clearly Sebastian had embarked on an extensive workout plan because it was now exceptional. But the most important muscle had remained the same and when it entered inside of me, time seemed to stand still.

Blair

"You haven't spoken a word to me the entire ride home," I said, once we arrived at Kirk's place.

"I was trying to get my thoughts together," he answered.

"It's been a few days now, you still don't know what to say?"

"Not really. I thought I did, but clearly I was wrong," Kirk stated, tossing his keys down before walking towards the kitchen.

I bit down on my bottom lip, completely freaked out by the conversation I knew we had to have, but I wanted more than anything to avoid. I wasn't ready to admit the truth because I wanted to create this idyllic situation with Kirk and I knew after we talked that would all change.

"I want you to know that the last few weeks have been some of the best times of my life. Living here with you, I felt like we were going to be the perfect family."

"If you thought everything was gonna be so perfect, why didn't you tell me you were pregnant?" he asked closing the refrigerator. "Is it because you know that's not my baby?" Kirk questioned, before taking a sip of water.

"No! It might be your baby, but I'm not sure," I blurted out. I immediately hated the way that came out but it was too late.

"So you were having sex with me and that..." Kirk couldn't even bring himself to say Skee's name, "at the same time," he finally said without actually saying Skee's name.

"It wasn't like that at all. When we started dating and we became intimate my intention was to only be with you and see if we could make our relationship work."

"But you what, found yourself back wit' that nigga in his bed?"

"No," I said shaking my head. "Honestly I don't know how I ended up in bed with Skee."

"Excuse me?" Kirk frowned.

"I know you'll probably think what I'm about to say is bullshit but it's the truth."

"Just say it, Blair."

"The next morning after we had spent the night together, Skee sent me a text asking would I meet him for lunch. He said he wanted to talk. So I met him for lunch and I had one drink. The next thing I know I woke up in his bed naked. He said we had sex, but I don't remember. I believe he drugged me, but he denies it. That doesn't matter now because I'm pregnant and either one of you could be the father. Kirk, you have to believe that I'm telling you the truth. I would've never had sex with Skee, especially not right after that amazing night we shared together. I was mortified when I woke up in his bed."

"So you moved in with me knowing that you were pregnant and wasn't sure who the father of the baby was," Kirk stated with a look of disgust on his face.

It took me a moment to respond because as I soaked in what Kirk said, shame flooded me.

"I wanted you to be the father of my baby so bad, that I guess in my mind I believed I could somehow make it come true."

"No, what you believed was that you could pass that baby off as mine. We would be living together for a couple months and then one day you would pretend you have this great news, that you were pregnant and I was the daddy. I'm sure you had it all figured out, but you didn't count on almost falling over a rail and your homegirl putting your pregnancy on blast."

"Kirk, it wasn't like that. I really wanted us to be a family."

"You do know I would've gotten a paternity test regardless. So your little scheme wouldn't have worked."

"This wasn't a scheme. It wasn't my intention to get pregnant. And when I did find out, I honestly considered not having the baby under the circumstances. But I want this child. This is my baby and it could be our baby."

"And it could be Skee's baby too," Kirk said with contempt in his eyes.

"Don't look at me like that."

"Like what? A woman who I believed I had a future with only to find out she deceived me."

"What can I do to make this right?" I asked.

"For one, move out," Kirk stated, tossing his bottle of water in the trash.

"You want me gone?"

"What? You think you can stay here with me, when there's a strong possibility you're carrying another man's baby."

"The baby also might be yours."

"Yeah and it might not and until I know for sure then it's best that we don't see each other."

"So it's over between us?" I questioned, choking up.

"Blair, what do you expect from me? From day one there has always been some bullshit with you. First that nigga, Michael, then Skee. I'm tired and fed the fuck up."

I was tempted to break down and burst out crying right on the spot, but I held back. I was beyond hurt. It was the sort of pain that I hadn't felt before, but in the mist of all my despair I didn't want Kirk's pity. I had made some poor choices and he had every right to be pissed. Although I hoped he would've been a little more compassionate and given me a break, I couldn't blame him for shutting me out.

"I'll have someone come pick up my things later," I said, placing the key to Kirk's place on the table and walking out. There was so much more I wanted to say, but I knew I couldn't pretend to be strong any longer. Once I closed the front door, I stood and cried my heart out for what felt like forever.

I woke up craving buttermilk pancakes. Before my pregnancy I wasn't a big breakfast person, but now I seem to want it everyday, all day long. I got out of bed and headed towards the kitchen. It wasn't a real kitchen, more like a tiny box with a stove and refrigerator. But I couldn't complain, at least it was mine for now.

After Kirk kicked me out, I went and stayed with Kennedy for a while. Although she said I was more than welcomed to stay for however long I wanted, I felt I needed my own space. I was about to be a mother and I couldn't sleep on Kennedy's couch for the rest of my life. I decided I needed my own place, but finding something decent in the city for a reasonable price was damn near impossible. But I lucked out and got a sublease from a model I had worked with in the past, who was going to Paris for a year to work. Besides the tiny kitchen, the apartment was actually really cute. There were lots of windows, which meant great sunlight. The ceilings were high with a lot of open space. It was also located in a great location. No, it couldn't compare to the likes of Skee's or Kirk's place but I was actually very content.

I turned some music on and began fixing some pancakes. Singing along to the Whitney Houston song playing in the background, I almost didn't hear the knock at the door. I turned the music down and walked over to the door and looked through the peephole.

"What are you doing here and how did you find out where I was living?" I asked Skee when I opened the door.

"Can I come in?"

"Sure," I said, stepping to the side so he could come in. "Now can you answer my question?"

"Blair, you know I can find out anything, but you should've told me anyway. I'm concerned about you. I want to be able to check up on you," Skee said, sounding sincere.

"I appreciate that, but I really needed some time to myself. You know, to think, try and figure things out."

"I understand, but you're pregnant and right now you need all the support you can get. Let me be here for you."

"You're being awfully considerate, especially when there's a chance the baby I'm carrying might not even be yours."

"It doesn't matter, Blair. I care about you. Regardless if this baby is mine or not, that won't change. I still can't believe Kirk just put you out like that," Skee added.

"Don't go there, Skee."

"I'm just saying. A woman in your condition shouldn't have to worry about having somewhere to sleep."

"I'm pregnant not bedridden. Plus, as you can see I have someplace to rest my head."

"Yeah, it's decent," Skee commented, looking around the apartment. "Not exactly where I would want the mother of my child resting her head but..."

"Again, Skee, we don't know if this is your baby or not."

"I get that but I would like to know."

"You're going to have to wait a few more months," I remarked going into the kitchen to finish making my food.

"You know there are tests you can take right now and find out. We don't have to wait," he said, walking right behind me. I knew Skee was correct because I had already spoken to my doctor about it. For the last few weeks I had been debating it back and forth in my head. Part of me wanted to take the paternity test now, so I could know who the father was and we could all move forward. The other part of me wanted to wait because once the results came in everything would be final. That scared me.

"There's no reason to be afraid, Blair," Skee stated, as if reading my mind.

"What makes you think that I'm afraid?" I stuttered, being caught off guard by his statement.

"I know you. I also know this would be difficult for any woman to deal with. But I think for all of us it would be better if we found out now instead of waiting until after the baby is born."

"Why the rush?" I said, reaching for the syrup and pouring it over my pancakes.

"You don't need to go through this pregnancy alone. And the sooner you know who the father is, either myself or Kirk can step up and take care of you the way you deserve. I'm not gonna lie, I want this baby to be mine. But if it's not, I'll have to accept that and move on."

"You're right. We're all at a standstill right now. It does make sense to find out which one of you is the father."

"Does that mean you're going to take the paternity test?"

"Yes. I need to know who's the father of my unborn baby once and for all."

Diamond

"Have you decided what you're going to order?" I asked Cameron, as I browsed over the menu.

"Nope, I'm still looking. What about you?"

"I think I'll have either the salmon or lamb," I said, taking a sip from my third glass of champagne.

"Both of those sound good," Cameron said, keeping his eyes glued to his menu. I couldn't put my finger on it, but something about him seemed off. We seemed to be back on track a few weeks ago, but then he started becoming distant again. It was so weird. I was blaming it on the poor season his team was having, but something in my gut was saying it was something else.

"Baby, is everything okay with you?' I questioned, feeling a little lightheaded from the bubbly. I reached my hand across the table and laid it on top of his.

"Everything is fine. Why do you ask?" he responded casually, but not making eye contact with me.

"You seem to have a lot on your mind and I want to make sure you're good. You know if..."

"It's Cameron Robinson. Hey man, can I get your

autograph?" a guy who seemed to be no more than 21 asked, interrupting me.

"No problem." Cameron smiled, signing the napkin the guy handed him.

"Oh and congratulations," a woman who I assumed was the man's date smiled and said to Cameron. Her comment felt so weird and for some reason I couldn't let it go.

"Congratulations for what?" I asked. The woman gave Cameron an awkward glance and then looked directly at me.

"On his baby," the woman said, without blinking. All the color in Cameron's face seemed to disappear. The man getting his autograph could see that Cameron had instantly become agitated. He seemed to be completely taken aback by what the woman said. He quickly took the napkin and grabbed the woman's arm, rushing her off.

"Wait!" I screamed out, but the man had whisked her away so quickly that by the time I had stood up out my chair she was gone. "What the hell is that woman talking about... what baby?" I questioned, feeling my heart racing.

"Diamond, calm down."

"Why in the fuck would that woman say some messy shit like that?"

"You know how some people can be."

"Yeah, I do, but you still ain't answering my question."

"Can we just order our food please," Cameron said, trying to disregard my concern and sweep it under the rug but I wasn't having it. I picked up my phone, went to Safari and searched does Cameron Robinson have a baby on the way. And just like that, to my horror all sorts of stories popped up. I kid you not; I fell out my chair due to shock.

"Diamond, let me help you up," Cameron said, rushing over to me. But I couldn't get my balance and honestly at that moment, I preferred staying on the floor. I didn't want to get up. My heart felt heavy as if any movement would cause it to leap out my body.

"Please tell me these are all lies," I said breathing hard. I closed my eyes wondering how I missed all the gossip. But then I remembered that Destiny had been sick and I was taking care of her. Once she got better I caught her virus so I was lying in bed, out of it. So I hadn't been on the blogs staying up to date on the latest gossip. As a matter of fact, this was really the first time I had been out since Cameron had taken me out on the town a few weeks ago in what I thought was us celebrating getting our marriage on track.

"Baby, here drink some water," Cameron said, handing me a glass as he helped me to my seat. I could barely take a few sips because my hand wouldn't stop shaking.

"Tell me these stories that are popping up about you having a baby on the way are all lies," I said, holding up my cell phone.

"Come on, let's go. This isn't the place for us to have this conversation," Cameron said, calling the waiter over to pay for the bottle of champagne before leaving.

It took me a few minutes to get up out my chair. The fact Cameron said we needed to have a conversation meant there was some truth to the gossip. I didn't want it to be true. I wanted Cameron to tell me there was no way he could have a baby on the way because I was the only woman he had been with, that I was his wife and he loved me and would never cheat.

"I think I'm gonna be sick," I said before running towards the bathroom to vomit.

When I woke up in the morning, I sat up in bed and watched a still sleeping Cameron. After leaving the restaurant I was so distraught and somewhat tipsy that we didn't even discuss what I had found out. Cameron insisted we both go to sleep and talk about it the next day when my mind was clear. It was the next day but my mind was no clearer. I needed answers and only Cameron could give them to me.

"Wake up... wake up," I said, shaking Cameron. He was a deep sleeper so I kept shaking. "Cameron, wake up."

"What's wrong... is everything okay?" he asked mumbling, half-awake and half-sleep.

"You need to wake up so we can talk," I insisted.

"Just a minute," he said, shifting his body over to go back to sleep.

I got out the bed and opened all the curtains so the sun beamed into the darkened bedroom. I could hear Cameron moan something, putting the pillow over his face, but the bright sunlight made it impossible for him to go back to sleep. He tossed the pillow down in frustration and headed to the bathroom. I sat on the edge of the bed, anxiously waiting for him to come out.

"What do you want me to say?" Cameron said, when he came out.

"I want you to tell me the truth. You've been acting different these last few weeks. I thought it had something to do with basketball, but now I know that's not the reason at all."

"You're right," he said, sitting down next to me on the bed and putting his head down. He had his hands on top of his head and kept shaking it back and forth. "I knew we had to have the conversation, but I avoided it because I didn't want to see that pain on your face.

"So it's true? You're having a baby with another woman!" I screamed out as I lost all control and the tears started flowing.

"Please calm down, Diamond," Cameron pleaded, reaching his hand out to me.

"Don't touch me! How could you do this? You know how much I wanted us to have a baby together and you go out and have a baby with another woman. How could you do this to me... to us!" I belted.

"You're right. When I found out about all the lies and I thought our marriage was over I fucked up and slept with a woman I used to deal with before we got together. I hate myself for it. Shit ain't been right with me since I found out."

"When is the baby due?"

"I'm not sure. Sharon, has been real vague with me."

"Sharon, that's her name." I swallowed hard knowing that I would now forever hate the name Sharon.

"Yeah."

"You're sure the baby is yours?"

"She's adamant it is. Of course I'll have a DNA test, but she wants to wait until after the baby is born."

"Has she asked you for any money?"

"Not yet but I'm sure it's coming. I already have my attorney on alert."

"So everybody knew about this baby. Wow, the joke really is on me."

"Diamond, nobody looks at you as a joke. I'm the one who fucked up. I let you down. I let our family down. I'm so sorry. I only pray that one day you'll forgive me."

"Forgive you. If only it was that easy."

"I'm still in love with you and I want our marriage to work. I know that might seem impossible to you right now, but please don't make any decisions about our marriage right now."

"That's the thing, Cameron. You've already made the decision about this marriage for us," I said, before walking out the bedroom.

Kennedy

"These last few weeks have been some of the best of my life." I smiled at Sebastian.

"I feel the same way," he said, stroking the side of my face. "Spending all this time together made me realize that the love between us is still there and I want us to try and make this work. I hope you want it to work too. Do you?"

"You didn't have to take me out to lunch to tell me this. Actually, I would've preferred if we had this discussion at your hotel room in bed." I giggled.

"I thought we needed a change of scenery. We seem to spend all our time in bed."

"True, but we had a lot of catching up to do." I grinned. "But to answer your question, of course I want this to work. This is the happiest I've ever been. It feels like old times, only better."

"I feel the same way. I know things might be a little difficult since I primarily live in LA, but I'm in New York a lot and I can come see you and you can come see me."

"You know it and maybe eventually I'll convince you to move to New York," I said.

"Or I can convince you to move to LA," Sebastian shot back. "Plus, it might be a little easier for you to make the move than me."

"Why is that?"

"My son lives in LA and I want to be near him."

"Your son... you have a son? You didn't tell me that."

"I'm telling you now. Knowing I have a child, does that change things?"

"Of course it changes things. You created this whole other life since we've been apart. It's like you erased me from your memory."

"Kennedy, that's not true. I thought about you every single day. Yes, I had a son who I love more than anything while we've been apart, but that never changed my feelings for you and definitely didn't erase what we shared from my memory," Sebastian stated.

"What about your son's mother, are you all still seeing each other?"

"Of course not. You know I don't get down like that, Kennedy. I'm a one-woman man. If I was still dealing with her I wouldn't be trying to be in a relationship with you."

"So what happened between the two of you? I mean, why did the two of you break up?"

"We were never an actual couple. She was someone I met a few months after I got out of jail and we became friends with benefits. The one time I forgot to wear a condom she got pregnant. Honestly, I tried to get her to have an abortion because I always planned on being married to the woman I had a baby with. She insisted on keeping the baby and I'm glad she did. He's the best thing that ever happened to me. Knowing I was going to be a father made me bust my ass and make something of myself. I give him the credit for all my success."

"What's his name?"

"Dylan."

"That's cute. I'm sure he's adorable."

"He is. I hope you'll meet him one day soon."

"Listen, I have to go. I'm late for a meeting," I lied and said.

"What meeting?"

"I totally forgot I have to meet with one of my clients at the office. Tammy just sent me a text asking me where I was."

"Okay, well call me later. I want to see you before I leave for LA tomorrow."

"I'll call you," I said, rushing out the restaurant. I jumped into the first taxi that stopped, desperate to get far away from that restaurant and Sebastian.

When I got back to the office to my surprise Diamond was there. "I thought you said you weren't coming in today," I said, sitting down at my desk.

"I needed to get out the house," she said in a low tone. It was so low I almost didn't hear her. I couldn't help but notice how disheveled she looked. Her hair was pulled up in a messy bun, she didn't have a drop of makeup on, not even some clear gloss. It appeared that Diamond had thrown on a t-shirt, some sweats and rolled out the house.

"Diamond, you don't look well. Are you okay?"

"No, my life is in complete shambles."

"What's wrong... is it Destiny, did something happen to her?"

"Destiny is fine. It's my marriage. Cameron cheated on me and the woman is pregnant."

"Gosh, I was hoping that wasn't true."

"You heard about it too?"

"Yeah, but I thought it was just a vicious rumor someone was spreading. Famous rich men like Cameron are always a target of malicious gossip. I didn't want to bring that unnecessary stress to you, especially when I wasn't sure if it was true."

"Well it is true and I don't know what I'm going to do."

"I thought what Sebastian just told me was bad but I can only imagine how devastating this must be for you," I said, feeling Diamond's pain.

"What happened with Sebastian?"

"He told me he has a son. He's not with his son's mother but..."

"Then what's the problem? It's not you all are married and he cheated on you and had the son. Kinda like what Cameron has done to me," Diamond smacked.

"I know that Cameron loves you and I also know that you love him too. What he did is fucked up, but I believe you all can get through it and keep your family intact."

"I wish you were right, but right now all I feel is betrayed and I don't know if I'll ever get over that."

"I understand."

"Thanks for listening to me vent, Kennedy, but I need to go pick up Destiny."

"No problem. If you need to talk, feel free to call me anytime. I'm here for you."

"I know and I love you for it. Thanks again," Diamond said, giving me a hug before leaving.

After Diamond left, I twirled around in the chair in front of my desk, daydreaming about Sebastian. Having him back in my life had me feeling better than I could've ever imagined, but with the news about his child and then the fact he lived in LA and we were so far apart made me rethink if our relationship really had a chance to survive. As all these thoughts played out in my head, I heard my phone ringing and it was Sebastian. I reached to answer it, but then I hesitated. I opted to let it go to voicemail. I wasn't sure if I was ready for love after all.

Blair

"Why is this happening to me?" I asked out loud, while having breakfast with Diamond and Kennedy at a quaint restaurant in the village.

"Why is what happening to you?" Diamond questioned, between bites of demolishing her French toast.

"Being pregnant and not knowing who the father is," I answered solemnly.

"Well, that's what happens when you have unprotected sex with more than one partner," Kennedy commented. She caught my glare as I cut my eyes at her. "I'm just saying." Kennedy shrugged, as she continued to eat her smoked salmon omelet.

"You know I didn't plan on having sex with Skee, hell I don't even remember it happening."

"And watch his ass end up being the father," Kennedy popped.

"Now why would you say that?" Diamond hissed, putting her fork down for the first time during the meal.

"I'm just being real. In situations like this, it's always the one you don't want to be the daddy that ends up being the papa. You all can stop looking at me crazy, 'cause you know I'm right."

"Who said that I didn't want Skee to be the father?" Blair said, causally.

"Hold up. First Kennedy talking crazy, now you, Blair. I thought you were over Skee and was hoping you could settle down with Kirk. When did that change?"

"Yeah, please explain. I too was under the impression that Kirk was your front runner for baby father," Kennedy mocked.

"At first I was hoping that Kirk would be the father but..."

"But what?" Diamond asked.

"Skee has been very sweet lately and on the other hand Kirk has been somewhat distant."

"He probably doesn't want to get attached to you or the baby until he knows if he's the father or not, which is understandable," Kennedy reasoned.

"Yeah, I think Kennedy is right. Cameron did mention that Kirk said he didn't even want to get excited about the possibility of you carrying his child until the test results came back."

"When are you going to get the test results?" Kennedy inquired.

"Should be any day now. I'm so nervous. As you can see I've completely lost my appetite," I said, looking down at my buttermilk pancakes that normally I would've devoured by now.

"Girl, you gotta eat for the baby," Diamond said, reaching over with her fork and taking one of my pancakes.

"Damn girl, aren't you hungry this morning," Kennedy joked. "But since we're sharing, let me get a bite of those pancakes too, 'cause they do look delicious. No sense in letting good food go to waste."

"The two of you are a mess. But enough about my baby drama because truth be told, it's already been determined who the father is and I can't worry over things I have no control over."

"Well isn't that a very mature thing to say," Diamond stated, as if surprised by my outlook on the situation.

"But Blair is right. Whoever's sperm traveled up through her uterus into the fallopian tubes and fertilized her egg is the baby daddy. That's how it works, plain and simple. So all the wishing in the world ain't gonna change the basics of what we learned in sex education class."

"We can always count on you not to sugarcoat anything, Kennedy."

"You're right about that, Diamond. But since you've dissected my relationships, why don't we talk about what's going on in your love lives," I said, eyeing both Kennedy and Diamond.

"Don't look at me," Diamond said, rolling her eyes. "I'm barely on speaking terms with Cameron. I don't know if my husband is coming or going."

"I'm sorry to hear that, Diamond. I was hoping things would be better for the two of you by now," I said.

"So was I," Kennedy added. "So the baby is definitely his?"

"Honestly I don't even know. Last time we discussed it he said he wasn't sure. The woman is refusing to take a DNA test until after the baby is born. I don't know if she just enjoys dragging this shit out or if she knows that baby might not be his. But real talk, the damage has already been done."

"Are you saying your marriage might not make it?" I asked.

"I don't know. Cameron and I have been through so much. We haven't had a chance to repair the damage that was done from the initial lies I told him about my past and the drama surrounding Rico. Now we're about to bring a potential outside baby into the mix. Jesus fix it, is all I can say." Diamond sighed, shaking her head. "Can we stop talking about my dismal situation? It's making me depressed the more I speak. Kennedy, why don't you fill us in on what's going on between you and Sebastian," Diamond said.

"Honestly, not much. I think it might be too late for us. Sebastian has a child and he lives in LA. I don't know where I would fit into his life."

"Sounds like a bunch of excuses to me. He is not with the mother of his child, last I checked New York has direct flights to and from LA so what are you really afraid of?" Diamond questioned.

Kennedy put her head down, not answering Diamond's question. Kennedy was never at a lost for words so I was surprised that she seemed to be shutting down. We both continued to stare at her but got nothing. Kennedy was on complete mute.

"You must really love him," I finally said, putting and end to the silence. Kennedy lifted her head and had tears in her eyes.

"Yes, I do. I always thought I would be the mother of his first-born child. I guess a part of me feels like I was easily replaced," Kennedy shrugged. "And Diamond you're right, I am afraid. I'm afraid to give Sebastian my heart again and he turns around and breaks it," Kennedy admitted.

"The thing is, he already has your heart. There's always a risk when you fall in love, but the two of you have been given a second chance, don't let it slip through your fingers. Life is too short for regrets," I said.

"Ain't this some shit. Girl, being pregnant has all of a sudden given you good sense," Diamond cracked, making us all burst out in laughter.

As the three of us sat at our booth laughing, for a brief moment I forgot all about my pregnancy drama. I embraced spending time with my best friends and not worrying about the dilemma between me, Kirk, and Skee. I knew this feeling wouldn't last long so I savored every second of it.

For the last couple days I seemed to be sleeping later and later, but I welcomed it because all the extra rest seemed to be a great stress releaser. As I laid in the bed for a few more minutes before getting up, I felt what at first seemed like a combination of butterflies, nervous twitches or a tumbling motion in my stomach. Then I realized the flutters were actually my baby moving.

"I can't believe you're moving," I beamed, as the biggest smile came across my face. I rubbed my stomach and a single tear rolled down my cheek as the realization that my baby was growing inside of me. It amazed me that I was so in love with someone that I had never laid eyes on or even touched. As I continued bask in feeling my baby move, I heard my cell phone ringing.

"Hello," I answered, almost knocking over the bottle water on my nightstand when I reached out for my phone.

"Hi, is this Blair?"

"Yes, who's calling?"

"This is Claire, from Doctor Crawford's office. The DNA results are in and we wanted to have you come in."

"Today?" I asked nervously.

"Yes, if possible. We've already contacted the other two parties and they're on their way." I swallowed hard unable to speak. "Blair, are you there?"

"Yes, I apologize. I accidently dropped the phone."

"So we'll see you here in the doctor's office, say in an hour?"

"I'll be there."

"Great, we'll see you soon, Blair."

The room seemed to start spinning after I hung up the phone. My initial reaction was to call Diamond and have her meet me at the doctor's office, but I decided against it. Although I was in desperate need of some moral support, I figured having Diamond there would make an already awkward situation even more awkward.

"Okay baby girl or boy, it's time to find out who your daddy is," I said out loud, patting my stomach as I headed to the shower. I continued talking as if the child growing inside of me could hear and understand everything I was saying.

"Kennedy, hi," I said, answering my cell, as I paid the driver before getting out the taxi.

"Hey you. I was just calling to let you know, that I followed your advice and I reached out to Sebastian."

"Really! That's awesome. How did it go?"

"Not sure yet, but I'm actually on my way to LA tomorrow for a weekend visit."

"I'm so proud of you, Kennedy. You're letting your guard down and taking a chance on love. That takes a lot of courage."

"It's because of you, Blair. You gave me that boost of confidence I needed. Thank you."

"My pleasure."

"How about you let me treat you to lunch today. We can go to that cute spot by your apartment. I can be to you in 20 minutes."

"That sounds great but can we make it a little later. There's something I have to take care of."

"Sure, is everything okay?"

"I'm standing outside in front of my doctor's office. The test results are in."

"Are you serious! You sound really calm. I can't believe you're not freakin' out."

"Trust me, part of me is. I'm keeping my cool though because I'm kinda relieved that we're finally getting this over with. In a few short minutes I'll know who the father of my baby is. One man will be a part of my life for a very long time and the other, more than likely won't."

"Do you want me to come up there?"

"No, I'm good. I do want us to do that lunch though." I laughed.

"You're handling this like a champ and yes we will be doing lunch. I'm going to call Diamond so she can join us. We have a lot to talk about."

"Cool. Do that and I'll hit you up as soon as I leave here."

"Great, talk to you soon."

I took a deep breath after I hung up with Kennedy, and after exhaling I opened the door to the doctor's office. The first thing I noticed was Kirk and Skee sitting down in the waiting room. They were seated across from each other, but it was obvious they weren't engaging in any conversation.

"Hi," I said, greeting both men with a cheerful smile. I was trying to bring some sunshine to a dismal energy in the air. I hadn't spoken to either of them in the last couple days and neither seemed happy to see me.

"How are you feeling?" they both asked simultaneously. When they realized they said the same thing, they gave each other a smug look then glanced back at me.

"I'm good. I just want to say one thing to both of you before we go in the doctor's office for the DNA results. I know this situation isn't ideal, but whichever one of you turns out to be the father of my unborn baby, I hope we can work together and be the best parents possible for our child. The life that's growing inside of me is innocent and deserves nothing but unconditional love."

"I agree," Kirk said, nodding his head.

"So do I," Skee chimed in.

"I'm glad you both..." before I could finish my sentence we were interrupted.

"Doctor Crawford is ready to see the three of you," the nurse said. "Please come with me."

We all followed behind the nurse and my heart was beating so hard, I just knew everybody could hear it. The walk down the hall towards her office seemed like the longest stroll of my life.

"Good afternoon, please everybody have a seat," Dr. Crawford said, giving us a pleasant smile. "I'm sure this is very stressful for all of you so I'm not going to make you wait any longer," she said opening up a manila folder. "Blair, the father of your baby is…"

Diamond

"If I have to read about this trifling home wrecker one more time, I'ma shoot somebody. Preferably her," Diamond sulked, tossing her iPhone down on her desk.

"Why do you torture yourself and read that garbage?" Kennedy questioned.

"Umm, it's my job to check the blogs... we are in the PR business, remember!" I shot back, annoyed by Kennedy's question.

"I'ma give you a pass on your sassy mouth because I know you're going through a difficult time, but please remember I'm not the enemy."

"I know," I sighed. "But besides you and Blair, I have to pretend with everyone else that I'm totally in control of the situation. So when we're together, I just let go and say everything I feel," I huffed, twirling around in my chair. "I do want to shoot her. I am tired of seeing her face, but it's like I can't escape it. I don't want to stop living my life and what I enjoy doing just to avoid another post about Cameron's maybe baby mama."

"I get that, but sometimes you have to avoid certain things just so you can have some sort of peace of mind."

"I won't be able to begin having any sort of peace until we get a DNA test and I know if that baby is Cameron's or not," I admitted.

"Well, she's only six months so you have a few more months to go."

"Don't remind me. This troll is using every moment of her pregnancy to get some shine. I wouldn't be surprised if she has cameras in the delivery room so she can share that with the world too. I mean where is the decency. She's proud that she's pregnant with a married man's child."

"Yep, especially when that married man is a multi-millionaire NBA player," Kennedy remarked.

"What I want to know is how is she getting all this press. Is she just randomly sending out pictures and press releases and all these blogs are biting. At this rate nobody will need a publicist, they can do it themselves."

"Actually she does have a publicist. She's not making all this magic happen on her own."

I stopped twirling in my chair and firmly placed both my heels on the floor before leaning forward. "Wait a minute. 'THOT' has a publicist. Who would stoop so low as to rep her?"

"Take a guess," Kennedy said rolling her eyes.

"Girl, I can't even begin to come up with a name. I mean who would stoop so low as to rep that trash."

"Darcy."

"Your Darcy!"

"She is not my Darcy... but yes, Darcy Woods."

'What a loser!" I screamed, tossing the ink pen I had in my hand across the room. "The nerve of that woman. Giving that home wrecker a platform to be heard."

"I know and Darcy is loving every minute of it. She knows we're friends and business partners so she feels like she's sticking it to me, too."

"I don't know how much more of this bullshit I can take," I snapped, reaching for my purse. "I need to run a few errands. I'll be back in a couple of hours," I said, wanting to get out of the office and get some fresh air.

"Do you want me to come with you... keep you company?" Kennedy offered.

"No, I wouldn't be much fun."

"Diamond, I know it doesn't seem like it right now, but things will get better."

"Yeah, 'cause they can't get no worse," I said, walking out the door. As I headed to my car, images of the 'other' woman's face kept flashing in my head. Those pictures of her on the blogs, holding her belly with that big fuckin' smile on her face like she had hit the jackpot. It was all too much for me to stomach.

"Diamond Robinson," I heard someone say, snapping me out of my thoughts.

"Yes," I answered, looking up to see two tall white men in cheap looking suits standing in front of my car.

"I'm Detective Reid and this is Detective Arnold. We need you to come down to the police precinct with us and answer some questions."

"Questions about what?" I asked, immediately feeling uneasy.

"The murder of Rico Grimes."

"You can give me the address and I'll meet you there."

"That won't be necessary. Our car is parked right behind yours." The office motioned his head towards their vehicle. "Now please come with us."

I had no idea what questions the detectives planned on asking, but my gut told me not to resist. The last thing I wanted was to come across as if I was guilty of something or had anything to hide. So without saying anything further, I followed the detectives to their car. I wanted to appear cooperative, but I also had my attorney on speed dial in case things quickly took a turn for the worse.

Kennedy

After Diamond left I kept thinking about what she said. I hated seeing her so miserable and although Cameron should've kept his dick in his pants, I felt it was beyond lowdown for Darcy to help his side chick rub it all in my girl's face. Enough was enough so I decided I was going to pay my ex-boss a visit as soon as I finished replying to a few important emails.

"Look what came for you," I heard Tammy say in a chipper voice, as I hit the send button. When I glanced up she was holding a huge bouquet of flowers.

"Those are for me?" I gasped in total shock.

"Yes! Aren't they gorgeous? You lucky girl, they were just delivered," Tammy said, handing the flowers to me. I placed them on my desk before sitting down to read the card:

Kennedy,

I enjoyed your visit to LA and I'm looking forward to you coming back. Hope it will be soon because I'm missing you already.

Love,

Sebastian

"Girl, you over there blushing hard as hell! That means those flowers aren't from a very pleased client, but from a very pleased man. I'm putting my money on Sebastian." She laughed. "Am I right?"

"Yes, Tammy, you're right," I said, admiring the gorgeous cut purple Vanda orchids, which were simply arranged in a novelty cobalt blue vase. They reminded me so much of Sebastian's taste, understated, but very expensive.

"I knew it, girl. I like his style. I've never seen purple orchids before," Tammy commented, leaning down to smell the flowers. "So are you going to call and thank him?"

"Yeah, but not right now in front of you, oh nosey self," I sniped, causing us both to laugh. "Hold the office down. I'll be back later."

"First Diamond, now you. I guess don't nobody feel like working today."

"Bye, Tammy. You can reach me on my cell if anything important comes up," I said before hauling ass.

I wanted to catch Darcy before she left her office. I remembered from the few years of me being her personal slave that every Wednesday she had a spa appointment at two o'clock. That gave me 20 minutes. Not wanting to take a chance getting caught in traffic, I decided to catch the A train downtown instead of hailing a cab.

I was eyeing my watch the moment I stepped onto the elevator at Darcy's office building. My train ride took longer than I expected and I was literally on borrowed time. When I reached Darcy's floor and the elevator doors opened, a huge relief came over me when her face was the one greeting me.

"Just the person I wanted to see," I said, stepping off the elevator and blocking the entrance so Darcy couldn't get on.

"Move out the way!" she belted, but the doors closed. "You're going to make me late for my spa appointment. Now move it!"

"I'm not going anywhere until we talk. So we can either have this conversation on our way to the spa together or we can go into your office. It's up to you." Darcy gave me the look of death before turning on her heels and heading towards her office, with me in close proximity.

"What do you want, Kennedy?" she questioned, slamming the door behind me.

"I want this dog and pony show you have that slut performing to come to an end... now."

"I thought Diamond was your friend? That's horrible to speak of her husband that way," Darcy sneered, leaning against her desk with folded arms.

"Last I checked, Cameron isn't your client that Sharon heffa is."

"Since you want to check me, let's do some fact-checking. Fact one, my client isn't married, but Cameron is. Fact two, my client didn't cheat on your friend, but her husband did. Fact three, if Cameron would've at least wrapped his dick up, I wouldn't have the ammunition to put on this dog and pony show you speak of. The bottom line, don't blame me for Cameron fucking up his marriage or my client. That culpability falls solely on his shoulder."

"No one is saying that Cameron is blameless in this situation, but spreading your legs for a married man isn't something to be proud of. For you to have this woman giving interviews like she's Michelle Obama is despicable. The next thing we know you'll be pitching her for the cover of *Essence* Magazine."

"That's already in the works, we're just waiting for Sharon to give birth. You know a mommy and baby cover. Those always sell well."

"I see. Well you do that and I guarantee Sharon will be the last client you ever have."

"Excuse me, Kennedy. Did I hear a threat? You're in no position to threaten anybody, especially not me."

"That's where you're wrong. I already know your client list is slowly dwindling over here. Things aren't what they used to be, especially since I left and took quite a few of your clients. I also know that Sebastian is paying a substantial monthly fee for your services. He's probably the biggest financial client you have at the moment and I promise you he'll be the first to go."

"You're a very funny girl, Kennedy." Darcy laughed.

"The only funny part is, I'm not joking."

"I find it humorous you believe that because of your past fling with Sebastian you still hold some clout with him. He's a businessman. Sebastian isn't going to allow you to fuck up what he's establishing right now because your little friend Diamond is in a frenzy over her husband knocking up my client. Not gonna happen. If you came all the way over here to tell me that, then you wasted a trip."

"Let's revisit that fact-checking you were doing earlier. Fact one, my dealings with Sebastian isn't a past fling, it's more like a current relationship. Fact two, yes Sebastian is about his business, that's why when he fires your ass, I already have Mark McKenzie's PR firm lined up to take over where you left off. I would take on Sebastian as a client myself, but I prefer not to mix business with pleasure. So I won't be fucking up anything. As a matter of fact, I'll be upgrading my man."

"You conniving bitch! You know how much I despise Mark and I can't believe Sebastian was stupid enough to rekindle a relationship with you, a serious one at that. You really disgust me!"

"The feeling is mutual." I smiled. "Darcy dear, we could swap name calling all day, but I have much more important things to do and I'm sure at this point you're desperate to make your spa appointment. So what's it going to be? Are you going to put a muzzle on that circus act client of yours or will I be placing a call to Sebastian?"

"Fine, I will cool things down with Sharon's PR campaign—"

"Not cool, put it on ice... permanently," I said, interrupting Darcy.

"Fine," Darcy shot back through clenched teeth. "But understand something, Kennedy. I can put a muzzle on Sharon, but it still won't change the fact that Cameron has a baby on the way. The damage in that marriage is done."

"Maybe you're right. But at least Diamond doesn't have to relive it every time she opens up a gossip magazine or reads a blog and has to see your client's face, grinning from ear to ear. Maybe without the constant reminder from the smear campaign you've orchestrated, Diamond's marriage might have a chance of surviving this disaster."

"I seriously doubt it, but that's no concern of mine. I'll keep my end of the bargain just make sure you do the same. Because, Kennedy, if you fuck up my business relationship with Sebastian, I will be out for blood... yours. Now please, get out of my office."

"My pleasure," I beamed, before making my exit.

Blair

I stood on the balcony of my apartment rubbing my stomach with the cool breeze whisking against my face as the sun brought the perfect balance of warmth. I closed my eyes as the wind blew through my hair and I lit up with a bright smile, as I felt my baby boy kicking my belly.

Feeling my son growing inside of me, gave me more pleasure than I ever thought possible. It was the closest thing I ever felt to unconditional love. Knowing that I had that gave me the strength to deal with the pain of his father not wanting to have anything to do with me. I walked back inside my apartment and sat down on the couch, before reaching for a glass of apple juice sitting on the table. My mind drifted back to a few weeks ago when the doctor revealed the paternity test.

Dr. Crawford looked over at Kirk and Skee before focusing her attention back on me. Her stare was serious and made me very uncomfortable. I almost didn't want to hear the results, but before I could yell stop, my child's father had been revealed.

"Blair, the father of your baby is Mr. McKnight."

"Are you sure?" he asked, as if not believing it was true.

"Positive. The results are in and they are accurate," Dr. Crawford assured him.

"Congratulations, you're a lucky man," Skee said to Kirk before turning to me. "I hate things had to turn out like this, but I wish you the best, Blair. If you ever need anything, don't hesitate to call," Skee said kissing me on the cheek before walking out Dr. Crawford's office.

"I'm going to give you two some time alone. Blair, I'll see you at your next checkup, but feel free to give me a call if you have any questions before then."

"Thanks, Dr. Crawford."

"This doesn't change anything." Those were the first words Kirk said to me after Dr. Crawford left us alone in her office.

"Really? You're the father. I'm carrying your child. I would think that changes everything."

"The only thing that changes is now I'll have to pay you child support. I'll have my attorney get in touch with yours, since I'm sure you already have one on deck."

"Wow, that's a low blow, even for you. You can't possibly think this baby is about a check for me?"

"Blair, I don't put anything past you anymore. You just got lucky that your initial plan worked out and I'm actually the father of your child. But I got lucky too. Because instead of you getting away with your lying and scheming, I found out the truth. So I will take care of my child, but you'll never fool me again. I know what type of woman you are. Like I said, my lawyer will be in touch. I'll be more than fair with the child support amount so try to keep it cute and not get too greedy. I don't need no baby mama drama with you dragging me in and out of court for more money. Let me know when the baby gets here," were Kirk's departing words.

I sat down in the chair in Dr. Crawford's office and cried my heart out for the next hour. Originally, all I wanted was for Kirk to be the father of my child, but never did I imagine it would come with such a heavy price.

"Thanks so much for meeting me for dinner. I know it was last minute but I needed to get out the house," I said to Kennedy when she sat down.

"Girl, no thank you! After the day I had, this is what I needed. What I need even more is a drink. Where's the waitress?" Kennedy asked, looking around for the lady that just brought us two glasses of water before disappearing.

"Rough day at the office?" I questioned, squeezing the lemon in my water before taking a sip.

"I had to go visit my least favorite person in this world. So that fucked up my entire day."

"You met with Darcy... why did you go visit that witch?"

"I'm impressed that you knew who I was talking about without me saying a word."

"I'm pregnant not senile, Kennedy."

"My fault." Kennedy laughed.

"So why did you go see her? It must have been awfully important."

"It was. Cameron's future baby mother is Darcy's client and she has that woman doing nonstop interviews. The shit was driving Diamond crazy so I had to put a stop to it."

"I'm sure that went nowhere being that the evil witch lives for other people's misery."

"Surprisingly, well, I'm not really surprised given the option I gave her. Being the level headed businesswoman that she is, Darcy agreed to put a halt to her shenanigans."

"Thank goodness, but you must've played one hell of a game with her. Congrats! But more importantly, I'm glad Diamond will get a minor break. This situation is taking a bad toll on her."

"Who you telling. I work with her everyday and I honestly started believing Diamond was about to start plotting somebody's murder."

"You know Diamond my girl, but I wouldn't put it past her," I joked but was somewhat serious.

"We got Diamond taken care of, at least temporarily so we good over there. My next question is how are you? Kennedy asked, giving me a suspicious glare. "Last time we talked all you told me was that Kirk was the father. Then I went out of town, but since I got back you've been very vague about everything. Are things better for you and Kirk now that he knows the child you're carrying is his?"

"You would think, but it's only gotten worse."

"Are you serious?"

"Very and it's breaking my heart," I admitted, not wanting to become emotional in the restaurant, but unable to help myself.

"I've been so worried about Diamond that I forgot all about you. I'm so sorry, Blair. It's just that Diamond's in my face complaining everyday because we work together and you've been quiet as a mouse. I figured all was good with you, not realizing you were just being strong, holding it all in. I feel awful," Kennedy said, placing her hand on top of mine.

"Don't feel bad. Honestly, I wasn't ready to share my feelings with anybody because I was trying to figure them out myself. In my mind I figured that once we knew who the father was, miraculously all would be right in my world. Boy was I wrong. But it was stupid for me to think that somehow Kirk would instantly forgive me if he turned out to be the father. Instead he seems to hate me even more."

"Kirk doesn't hate you, Blair."

"Yes he does. He doesn't want anything to do with me. He says he'll pay child support, but I don't even think he wants a relationship with our child."

"Kirk is angry right now and although he doesn't want to admit it, he's hurt. Give him some time. He'll come around."

"I hope you're right because I have so much love to give and if I have to I will raise our child on my own, but I don't want to. I want our son to have a father."

"You're having a boy?"

"Yeah." I smiled. "You're the first person I told."

"Really! I feel super special. That lil' man is gonna be such a heartbreaker. I'm so happy for you, Blair," Kennedy said, giving me a hug.

"Thank you, if only Kirk felt the same way."

"He'll come around… trust me. How did Skee take the news?" Kennedy asked.

"Skee handled it really well. He's actually called me a couple times, you know just checking up on me. Making sure I didn't need anything."

"Dare I say, I'm impressed. I didn't expect Skee to take it well. I figured his ego would cause him to have a massive temper tantrum."

"Nope. I can't help but to think how different things would be right now if he turned out to be the father. I definitely wouldn't feel so alone."

"You're not alone, Blair. We've been a little preoccupied, but Diamond and I are about to step up on our daddy duties."

"You so silly," I said as we both giggled.

"Girl, I'm serious. Do you need anything? You know like some financial assistance until you and Kirk get everything worked out."

"Actually once the paternity results came back Kirk had his attorney immediately set up monthly payments. You know to cover all my pregnancy expenses and to help cover my bills."

"See, he's coming around already."

"Don't get me wrong I appreciate the financial support. It no doubt alleviates a lot of stress but..."

"But you much rather have his emotional support too," Kennedy said, finishing my thoughts.

"Exactly. Kirk made it clear he planned on supporting our child, but I hope eventually he'll contribute more than just a check."

"Have a little faith. Kirk will come around. In the meantime, all you need to do is focus on taking care of yourself and that bundle of joy growing inside of you."

"You're right. I have to be strong for my son," I said with confidence and that's what I planned on doing, starting now.

Diamond

"Detective Reid, I've been here for over two hours and I've answered all of your questions so can I go now?" I questioned, trying to keep my calm composure intact.

"Here's the thing, Diamond. Myself and Detective Arnold have listened to everything you said, and we both feel your holding some things back. Ain't that right Steve?"

"Yep, I have to agree with my partner. You seem to have all the right answers, but we're looking for the truth," Detective Arnold chimed in.

"That's all I've been giving you for the last couple hours."

"If that's true, then why do we have an eyewitness who can place you at the scene of the shooting?"

"Scene of what shooting?"

"Rico's shooting," Detective Reid replied as if slightly put off that I was pretending not to know what shooting he was talking about.

"Your eyewitness must be mistaken or is either lying because as far as I know I was nowhere near where

Rico got shot. But then again, I have no idea where he was shot."

"Is that right?"

"Yes, Sir. I hate that your witness's false information has sent you on a pointless goose chase. I wish I could be more helpful but I have nothing to add," I said rising up from my chair in the interrogation room.

"No so fast, Mrs. Robinson. Not only do we have a witness, what if I was to also tell you that a surveillance camera across from the alley where Rico was shot, has your car on camera with you behind the wheel."

I put on my best poker face determined not to show even the slightest bit of fear. I was almost positive that what Detective Reid said was all lies, but I wasn't taking any chances. I already sat and ran my mouth for two hours without lawyering up because I felt it was imperative for me to appear that I wanted to cooperate. I mean although it was no secret I loathed Rico, he was Destiny's father and if I was innocent, I would at least want to help the detectives find his killer for our daughter's sake. But since I really was the shooter, I could only take this cooperating act but so far before I ended up accidently further implicating myself.

"Listen, Detective Reid, I really want to help you... I really do. I've been extremely forthright, but you're beginning to make me feel very uncomfortable by saying things that I know are absolutely untrue. Because of that, if you have any more questions for me, I'm going to need for my attorney to be present. Do I need to get him on the phone?"

"That won't be necessary. You're free to go," Detective Reid said. Given the mean mug on Detective Arnold's face, clearly he was surprised by what his partner said.

"You gentleman enjoy the rest of your day," I said grabbing my purse before leaving. I wanted to run out the police precinct, but I took my time getting to the exit door as if I didn't have a care in the world. I was so cold with it that I almost convinced myself that I wasn't the real culprit.

It wasn't until I hoped in the cab and got back behind the wheel of my own car that I released my true feelings. "What the fuck!" I screamed out, pounding my fist on the steering wheel. "I thought that shit was done and buried but no, them motherfuckers are coming for me. I know Lela is behind this bullshit. She just can't let this shit go," I continued, shaking my head. This was the sort of agitation I didn't need right now. Between Cameron's maybe baby and a potential murder charge dangling over my head, my blood pressure had to be tipping on the dangerous level.

Right as I was about to pull off, I noticed Cameron was calling me. At first, I ignored the call because he was the last person I wanted to talk to, but he called back again.

"Hello," I answered with a funky attitude.

"Did I catch you at a bad time?" Cameron asked, recognizing my sharp tone.

"Sorta," I huffed, unable to shake my bad mood.

"I needed to ask you something."

"Ask."

"Well, I got a call from..." Cameron took a long pause that prompted me to jump in.

"A call from who?" I asked, wondering if those foul detectives reached out to Cameron fetching for info. I quickly got my story together to shut down whatever BS they told him.

"I got a call from Sharon."

"From who?" I questioned, making sure I heard Cameron correctly.

"Sharon," he repeated, clearing his throat. "Have you stepped to her with any sort of threats because she's threatening to sue us for harassment."

"Excuse me! I don't even know this woman, let alone how to get in touch with her. How the fuck would I step to her with some threats?"

"I had to ask. I haven't been in touch with her so I assumed it had to be you."

"Oh really? So you assumed I reached out to your sidepiece and threatened her. I can't believe you called me with this bullshit. You know what Cameron, go fuck yourself 'cause I don't need this bullshit right now," I yelled before ending the call. I cut my phone off, tossed it in my purse, and sped off.

When I woke up the next morning, I almost forgot I spent the night at the W Hotel. I was already on edge after being grilled by the detectives and after my conversation with Cameron I was done. I had no desire to go home or be around anybody.

Although Cameron pissed me off, the Sharon situation was no longer at the top of my priority list. I had a much bigger problem that had to be dealt with. I spent the night getting my thoughts together so I could decide how I would proceed. The common denominator with the

Rico fiasco was Lela. I was positive she was the one keeping his murder investigation on the front burner. I even believed she somehow came up with this fake witness to light a fire under the detectives. It was no coincidence that after all this time, this so called witness stepped forward with the new information. I also knew that the detectives weren't a hundred percent sure about the validity of the information because if they were I wouldn't be lying across a king size bed, instead I would be locked up in jail charged with murder.

As confident as I was that the police didn't have the smoking gun, I needed to get Rico's murder investigation closed once and for all. I had to move swiftly, but with caution. I placed a phone call to the one person who could help me out of this mess.

"Renny, I need to see you."

"Come now. I'll be waiting," he said, before hanging up. I took a quick shower, got dressed and rushed out to meet with Renny.

"Diamond, Diamond, Diamond, I thought you already used up all your favors," Renny said, when I entered his townhouse. It was his low-key spot that he used to conduct business such as this.

"I know it always seems I need something, but I'm good for it."

"Like you were last time, when you had to cut me off because your husband was breathing down your throat."

"Renny, I apologized for that and I hooked you up with somebody who was able to pick up where I left off.

You have to admit, I always come through for you just like you always come through for me."

"What is it that you want, Diamond?" he asked, not amused.

"The police are on me for Rico's murder."

"There is no surprise there. I told you not to commit that murder yourself," he said sitting down on the couch, turning on the television.

"You know why I had to kill Rico myself. I needed justice for what he did to me."

"Will that justice be worth it if you have to spend 25 years to life in jail?"

"That's why I need your help. To make sure that doesn't happen."

"What can I do?'

"Before he died, Rico told his girlfriend, Lela, that I was the one who shot him. Of course I denied it, but she's been telling anybody that will listen that I'm his killer. She even took it to the police but without any evidence they dismissed what she said."

"So what's changed?"

"Somehow she's come up with some fake witness who claims they saw me on the scene when Rico was shot."

"Are you sure she's behind it?"

"Positive. She even confronted me weeks ago when I was out shopping. Lela was adamant she was going to bring me down for Rico's murder. She won't let it go and I'm afraid she's going to keep coming up with shit until the police arrest me. If she was out the picture, I believe the case would go cold."

"So what, you want me to have her killed?"

"Ideally yes, but I know that might put me on the police radar even more."

"Then what?" Renny asked.

"I just want you to have your men scare the shit out of her. I want her to be so afraid that she packs her bags and gets the hell out of town for good. There's nothing here for her. I had my people do some investigating and she has no family here. They're all down south. She moved here for Rico. Now that he's dead she needs to take her ass back to Houston, the sooner the better."

"That's doable. Just give me all the info you have on her."

"No problem, but make sure your men know that I don't want her hurt. It's also imperative that she has no clue that I'm behind it. I don't want her to have anymore ammunition to take to the cops."

"I got you. But, Diamond, I hope after I clean up this mess you keep yourself out of trouble. This is becoming a pattern for you. I beginning to think you're addicted to drama."

"Trust me, I have a checklist and I'm working my way down. I'm trying to get rid of anything or anyone who means me harm and Lela is the first name on the list. I'm desperate for some peace in my life and I will get it."

Kennedy

"Girl, where have you been? Last time I saw you, you were going out for some fresh air. That was two days ago. You haven't been answering your phone or responding to text messages. I was about to report you missing," I said to Diamond when she walked in the office.

"Please forgive me, but that moment I needed got extended."

"Did something else happen?" I questioned, concerned by the drained look on Diamond's face.

"Yes. The police brought me in for questioning for Rico's murder. I know his girlfriend is behind it but I'm straight. It's frustrating though. Then Cameron called me about some dumb shit regarding the woman he knocked up."

"What about her?"

"He asked me had I threatened her because she said she was going to sue us for harassment."

"Get the fuck outta here."

"I wish, but I'm serious. I couldn't make this shit up. I don't even have that broad's number, how the hell can I threaten her with anything."

"I wonder if this has anything to do with my conversation with Darcy?"

"I know you said Darcy was her publicist, but what would she have to do with Sharon's claims of harassment?"

"After you left the other day I went to see Darcy."

"You did?" Diamond's eyes widened, wanting to know what we talked about.

"I told Darcy to end this publicity campaign she had that home wrecker on or I would have Sebastian drop her ass and take his business to a competitor that she detests."

"No, you didn't!" Diamond said, seemingly in shock, but grinning from ear to ear. "I can't believe you did that for me. You're the best!" she said, high fiving me.

"Of course I would do that for you. Not only are we business partners, but you're also one of my best friends. Plus, I immensely enjoyed serving shade to Darcy." We both laughed.

"That has to be why that Sharon chick called Cameron about to have a nervous breakdown. Her 15 minutes of fame had gotten cut short. The thirst is real for these hoes."

"You ain't lying. But I wonder what Darcy told her. She shouldn't have placed the blame directly on you and Cameron. That wasn't part of the..." before I could finish my sentence, Tammy came running in the office breathing heavily.

"What the hell is wrong with you?" Diamond and I asked at the same time.

"I would tell you to turn on the Wendy Williams show but the segment already went off. I was watching it at the nail salon next door and I rushed back over to tell you what she said."

"Girl, calm down and take a seat," Diamond said, taking Tammy's hand and sitting her down.

"So Wendy said something on her show?" I questioned, wanting Tammy to tell us what had her all riled up.

"Yes. On her Hot Topic segment, Wendy said that supposedly Cameron and his wife had his soon-to-be baby mama's publicist drop her as a client so she could stay out the press because it was making him look bad."

"Stop!" Diamond screamed.

"I know that's what I was saying the entire time the segment was airing. They even showed a picture of you and Cameron at some red carpet event, then a picture of Sharon, smiling, holding her pregnant belly."

"I'm going to kill Darcy. This has her spin written all over it," I seethed while dialing her number.

"This is Darcy," she said, answering her phone.

"Darcy, this is Kennedy. I just heard what Wendy Williams said on her show today. How did the conversation we have turn into you leaking lies to the media that Cameron and Diamond made you drop Sharon as a client?"

"Kennedy, I had absolutely nothing to do with that. After we spoke, I simply told Sharon that I could no longer represent her, nothing more."

"So this new angle the media is running with, came from where?"

"I have no clue. Maybe Sharon is making it up to create more buzz for herself. You know since I agreed not to get her anymore stories discussing her relationship with Cameron and her pregnancy."

"You expect me to believe that some gold digging hussy is media savvy enough to come up with a story like this on her own."

"I don't really care what you believe. We made a deal and I've been sticking to it. I expect for you to do the same. I can't control what my ex clients do," she mocked. "But, Kennedy, as much as I would love to entertain this conversation, I have another call. *Au revoir.*"

"Did that wrench just hang up on me," I said, looking at the phone in disdain before hanging up.

"At what point is this nightmare going to end," Diamond sulked.

"Diamond, I'm so, so sorry. Never did I think Darcy would stoop this low. But I promise, she will pay for this."

"Kennedy, this isn't your fault. You were looking out for me and Darcy flipped the script to further benefit her own agenda. But to outright lie on Cameron and me when we had nothing to do with it... wow, she truly is a snake. I wouldn't be surprised if Darcy actually told Sharon that version of the story just to get her extra amped up. That would explain why she felt the need to call Cameron. Damn, this is him calling me now," Diamond said, shaking her head.

"Aren't you gonna answer it?" I questioned.

"No. I don't feel like hearing his mouth. I'm sure he's heard about the show and that's what he's calling about. I'll talk to him when I get home."

"That Darcy is a piece of work. I remember all the shenanigans she used to pull when we worked for her," Tammy popped. "I'm so glad to be free of her madness and I have the two of you to thank for that."

"Well, Darcy finally picked the wrong person to try her shenanigans on," I said, twirling around in my chair.

"The nerve of her to lie on you and Cameron. If that girl Sharon really sues you all, I'm going to be..."

"Kennedy, stop," Diamond said, cutting me off. "Sharon has no bases for her lawsuit even if everything she said was true, that isn't harassment. She's just looking for a quick payday by embarrassing us even further. I guess those child support checks aren't enough, she need settlement/hush money too. These hoes ain't loyal."

"Diamond, don't worry it will all work out," I said, wanting to believe what I was saying was true. I felt so guilty and angry not only with Darcy but myself.

"Girl, listen, don't stress over this mess 'cause it's gon' do what it do. I have so much other shit on my mind that I'm starting to be over Sharon and my marriage."

"Don't say that, Diamond. Don't let this woman ruin your marriage," I pleaded.

"You're giving Sharon way too much credit. If anybody ruined my marriage it would be Cameron, although I've made my mistakes too. The point is the other woman, or whatever you want to call her isn't the reason my marriage is in shambles, it's because of me and Cameron, no one else."

"I hear you. I do hope you all are able to work things out. Even with all the drama going on, I know how much you love your husband and he loves you too. I wish I could snap my finger and make everything right between the two of you. I can't fix your marriage, but what I can do is make sure Darcy Woods gets what's coming to her and I plan on doing exactly that," I promised myself.

Blair

"Girl, I can't believe how big you've gotten, but you all belly," Diamond said, patting my stomach. "You look so beautiful pregnant."

"You know my due date is fast approaching and my stomach seems to have doubled in size overnight. But thanks for saying I look beautiful because that's the last thing I feel like. The only shoes my feet are comfortable in are flip-flops. I have them in all colors and designs. You know, so I can feel somewhat fashionable."

"I know how you feel. When I was pregnant with Destiny I ate everything in sight and couldn't fit nothing. All I wore was jogging pants and t-shirts. But look at you, you're all baby, your face hasn't even gotten bigger. And your hair has gotten so long and thick. You are having a boy. I heard boys give you beauty and girls take it away. I know Destiny took mine from me."

"Well clearly you got it back because you're more beautiful than ever."

"Thanks for saying that, Blair. I need all the compliments I can get. I might look like I have it together on the outside, but on the inside a bitch is hurting bad," Diamond admitted.

"Hopefully a good meal will help you feel better," I said when we walked into The Ainsworth, a restaurant in Chelsea.

"I came here a couple months ago for a product launch event with Cameron. I always wanted to come back for dinner because the hors d'oeuvres we had were delicious," Diamond said, before going over to the hostess so we could be seated.

"This place is really cute," I commented on the way to our table noticing the antiqued pine walls with aged mirrors and rustic chandeliers. There were also multiple hi-def televisions throughout the venue, so you would have an unobstructed view from wherever you were seated.

"I like the design too. It has the rustic chicness of the Chelsea Flower District mixed with the Manhattan party life feel. It's a nice combination," Diamond added.

"Let's hurry up and look over this menu. I'm starving and so is the baby because he just kicked me." I laughed.

"How cute is that. Although I got big as a house, I loved being pregnant. I was hoping by now I would be pregnant with my second child, but it looks like Cameron's plaything beat me to it."

"I hate that you're going through that."

"Me too, but let's not talk about my dreadful marriage. Let's talk about happy stuff like you and the baby. I know Kirk must be so happy you're having a boy."

"We haven't had one of our girl chats in awhile and obviously you and Cameron haven't been doing any pillow talking."

"True to both, but that's why we're having dinner so we can catch up, so back to Kirk. I know he was totally excited when you told him you were having a boy."

"Kirk doesn't know I'm having a boy because he doesn't talk to me." Diamond's mouth dropped wide open, but before she could say anything the waitress appeared ready to take our order.

"Did you ladies have a chance to look over the menu?"

"Yes, I want the marinated skirt steak," Diamond said.

"How would you like that steak cooked?"

"Medium well."

"And you Miss," she said, turning towards me.

"I'll take the Thai kale salad and a side of truffled mac and cheese."

"Thank you. I'll take those menus. Let me know if you need anything else," the waitress said with a warm smile before leaving.

"Now that we ordered our food and got that out the way, we can get down to business. You're telling me that even though Kirk knows he is the father of your unborn child, he's still not speaking to you?"

"Nope. He basically told me that I'm having this baby for a check. That he'll pay child support, but he doesn't want to have anything to do with me."

"That fuckin' asshole. I can't believe he would treat you like this. Did he forget that it was him that chased you? You didn't even want to date Kirk at first, now he's labeling you as some sort of gold digger. The nerve of him. He has truly pissed me off."

I couldn't help but find it humorous by how upset Diamond was.

"What's so funny... why are you laughing?" Diamond wanted to know.

"I find it cute and sweet by how upset you are."

"Aren't you upset? I mean you're the one that's pregnant."

"I was and yeah I'm still hurt, but I've accepted it and I'm moving forward. I have a baby to take care of and a son to raise. I can't let Kirk's attitude ruin what is supposed to be one of the happiest times of my life."

"No doubt, but that motherfucker is still foul. You make sure you drag his ass through the mud for child support. If you need money for an attorney I'll be more than happy to give it to you."

"Thank you, but that won't be necessary. The one thing Kirk did make clear was that he didn't want any baby mama drama. He's already started making payments and we've agreed on a child support amount. All that was very amicable and he was more than fair."

"As he should be. It ain't like you trapped that nigga. Sorry sonofabitch. You're giving that man his first child and he want to treat you like shit. How dare he."

"Listen, I'll be fine. I'm going to have my baby. Spend time with him, get my body back right so you and Kennedy can get me back working. There are a lot of successful single mothers and I'm going to be one of them."

"I'm loving your positive attitude. I hope you can keep it when you see who just walked in." Diamond frowned.

Without hesitation I quickly turned towards the entrance and my heart dropped when I saw Kirk come in with a woman on his arm. It didn't help my self-esteem one bit that his date was wearing a skintight dress showing that all her curves were in the right place. The crazy part was even with my swollen feet I had felt somewhat pretty when I left my apartment tonight. I put on a one-shoulder sleeveless maternity dress that I thought was super cute. It was a pink lemonade color with a cluster of rosettes at the shoulder and an asymmetrical neckline. It had an elastic waistband, allowing the skirt to flow down. It was so girlie and feminine. Although in my head I knew I was pregnant, seeing the sexy woman with Kirk made me feel like pudgy slob.

What made it even worse was that Kirk caught me staring at them. I felt like such a loser and quickly turned back around. "I can't believe this is happening," I said under my breath.

"Relax, Blair. This too shall pass," Diamond said, reading the anxiety all over my face.

"Hey, Diamond," Kirk said, speaking to her when he walked past our table, but Diamond didn't say a word back.

"You could've spoken to him."

"Until Kirk does right by you, I don't have shit to say to him. You're my best friend. Fuck that motherfucker."

"I love you, Diamond."

"I love you too, girl. Here comes our food now. So let's eat before Kirk ruins our appetite." We both burst out laughing before diving into our meals.

Diamond

"So you finally decided to come home," Cameron said when I walked through the door.

"I needed some time alone to think, for obvious reasons," I said, dropping my purse and keys on the table.

"How do you expect for us to work on our marriage if you won't even come home or answer your phone?"

"Is that what we're supposed to be doing, working on our marriage. That's news to me."

"So when I found out about all those lies you told me, I eventually forgave you because I wanted our marriage to work. You don't think you owe me the same thing?" Cameron asked.

"Me lying to you because I was ashamed of the life I had been living to take care of myself and my daughter is totally different than you having a baby on me while we're married. And like you said, you eventually forgave me. If I remember correctly you were the first one screaming for a divorce when you did find out about the lies. So I'm supposed to swallow my pride, hide my pain, and ride this out for you?"

"When we took our vows it was for better or for worse. I know I should've handled things differently when you came clean to me about your past. I was wrong and I can admit that. But remembering our vows is what brought me back."

"Was that before or after you knocked up Sharon?"

"I deserve that. You can say all the slick shit you want as long as you're home with me fighting to save our marriage. If you're not here, we're not gonna make it."

"That's the thing, Cameron, I don't know if I want us to make it."

"Why would you say that?"

"When you asked me to be your wife I felt so blessed like I was the luckiest woman on earth. You surpassed all my expectations from what I wanted in a husband. Honestly, I felt that I didn't even deserve you. Then after we got married, I couldn't wait to get pregnant. I was going to feel so honored to be the mother of your first-born child. But now you've robbed me of that."

"Diamond, we can still have a baby together. We can have as many as you want."

"Don't you get it, it won't be the same. Some woman that you used to have sex with and then started seeing again when we were having problems in our marriage is going to give you your first born child, not me, your wife. I don't think I can get over that."

"As much as we love each other, I know we can. You and Destiny are my life. I can't imagine living without the two of you in it."

"But it's just not us anymore. Another woman and a child are involved. The baby is going to deserve your love and mine too, but I don't think I'll be able to give it and that's not fair to your child. The baby is innocent, but my resentment towards you and the woman you got pregnant is going to make it impossible for me to embrace your child."

"I understand it's going to take you time to accept my child and I won't pressure you. The baby doesn't have to be around you until you're ready."

"I might never be ready!" I screamed.

"Baby, I don't have all the answers right now," Cameron said, taking my hand, "but what I do know is you're my wife and I love you more than anything, so we will make this work. But I can't fight for us on my own. I need you to fight too. Can you do that?"

"I don't know," I said, releasing my hand from his grasp.

"Think about our family and what we've built. No other man will ever love you as much as I do and there is no other woman I want to give my last name to, but you. Please don't give up on us. I'm begging you."

"I'm going to take a shower and go to sleep. We can talk about this some more another time," I said, walking away.

There was no denying my love for Cameron and my heart aching each time I thought about leaving him. But if I couldn't find a way to genuinely accept his child then I knew it would never work and our marriage was over. I needed to do some serious soul searching and figure it out because our future together depended on it.

As I headed down Broadway on my way to the office, I kept replaying the conversation I had with Cameron the night before. I was so deep into my thoughts that at first I didn't hear my cell phone ringing.

"Hello," I said, finally answering the call before they hung up.

"There was a slight problem," I heard Renny say over the phone.

"What happened?"

"My men were making a lot of progress shaking things up, but last night things went bad."

"Please tell me she's not dead," I said, feeling like my heart was about to jump out my chest.

"She's not dead, but she was involved in a very bad accident while one of my men was pursuing her. The driver lost control of the car and crashed into a pole. He died at the scene. I just got word that the man driving was her brother."

"Fuck!" I belted. "Your man wasn't caught, arrested, or anything was he?" I questioned, about to hyperventilate.

"No we're good on our end. But I thought you should know what happened. Do you want me to have my men shut things down for a minute?"

"Of course! Nobody was supposed to die."

"You and I both know there are no guarantees when it comes to things like this. It's unfortunate, but it happens. If you change your mind and want to start things back up let me know," Renny said then hung up.

After my call with Renny I had to pull over. I was beginning to think I was destined for a life full of drama. Even when I tried to clean up a mess it seemed like shit would only get messier. The only good thing was Lela had no idea I played a role in the car accident. If she knew I was responsible for not only Rico's death, but also her brother's she might say fuck the police and try to kill me herself.

Kennedy

"Sebastian, I'm so happy to see you," I said, wrapping my arms around his neck as he pulled me in for a long lingering kiss.

"Not as happy as me. I couldn't wait any longer for you to have time to come back to visit me in LA so I decided to come to you."

"Baby, I'm sorry, but things have been crazy on my end. But now that you're here, I'm going to make your trip worthwhile," I teased, unbuttoning his shirt. I led him to the bedroom in his hotel suite as we undressed each other.

"I can't wait to slide inside of you," Sebastian whispered in my ear, softly kissing my earlobe.

"Before you do I want to taste your dick in my mouth," I baited, bending down on my knees, draping my wet lips around his rock hard tool.

"Dammmmmn," was all Sebastian managed to say falling back on the bed, closing his eyes. I licked and sucked making love to his dick with my mouth like he was stroking inside my pussy.

Right when I felt his dick pulsating I stopped sucking so he wouldn't cum. I then slid on top and began riding his thick meat slowly but steady. Sebastian lifted up, cupping my breasts as his warm tongue took turns licking my hardened nipples.

"Ahhhhh," I purred, arching my back as my body savored every second of pleasure Sebastian was giving me. We seemed to make love over and over again and I welcomed it.

"You were unbelievable," Sebastian rolled over and said after finishing our final sex session.

"You were pretty amazing yourself." I smiled, nuzzling the tip of his nose. "Have I told you how happy I am to have you back in my life?"

"No, but you don't have to because I feel the same way. I get upset at myself sometimes for not coming back into your life sooner. There had been this void that I could never fill ever since I got out of jail. Now that you're back in my life, it's not there anymore."

"Baby, I know exactly what you mean." I leaned over and kissed Sebastian wishing we could stay in each other's arms forever.

"Since we're on the same page, when are you coming to live with me in LA?"

"You want us to live together?" That was the last thing I expected Sebastian to say.

"I do. So what do you say?"

"My company, business, and my friends are in New York. I don't know if I'm ready to up and leave that behind to start over in LA. Don't get me wrong I'm tempted because I would love to wake up to you everyday."

"Will you at least think about it? We've missed out on so much time together I don't want to waste anymore," Sebastian said.

"You're right. I can't make any promises other than I will think about it," I said.

"That's all I ask. No matter what you decide we'll make it work. Now that I have you back in my life I'm never letting you go because I love you."

"I love you, too."

"You know I hate leaving you, but when I told Darcy I was in town, she said she needed to discuss some important business with me. Hopefully it won't take long. Will you stay here and wait for me until I get back?"

"Of course."

"Feel free to order some room service. Get whatever you want. When I get back maybe we can go out to dinner."

"Or maybe we can stay in for dinner, watch movies, and make love all night," I suggested.

"I think I like your idea better."

"I knew you would. I have one more idea that I want you to consider," I said.

"Anything for you."

"I want you to fire Darcy."

"I know you dislike Darcy, but she's been doing a very good job. It wouldn't be a wise business decision to get rid of her. Did something happen recently between the two of you?"

"Yes and this time she beyond crossed the line. I really need you to do this for me. Plus, I already have someone that will be able to replace Darcy immediately.

Not only is he better, but he'll also do the job for half the price."

"Really?"

"Yes. His name is Mark McKenzie. Google him, you'll see he's the real deal."

"And you're sure about the price?"

"Positive, I've already spoken to him. But trust me, you'll be so pleased with his work you'll probably decide to give him a bonus anyway."

"He's that good?"

"Yep. I give you my word."

"You better be right," he said, giving me a kiss. "I'll let Darcy know today." Sebastian gave me his signature devilish grin then got in the shower.

"Let the takedown of Darcy Woods begin." I giggled, falling back in the bed.

"Tammy, can you bring me the Nike file. I need to verify some names for an upcoming event we have to do for them," I said, trying to get business in order. I wanted to start the week off being productive. Lately, I had been sidetracked with so many other outside problems that I felt like I was letting some things fall through the cracks.

"Here you go," Tammy said, handing me the file. "Do you need anything else?"

"This is all for now," I said, opening up the folder. "Who is this?" I asked out loud, putting the file down to answer my phone.

"I warned you not to cross me."

"Who the hell is this playing on my phone!"

"You know who the hell this is," the woman snapped.

"Darcy Woods. What took you so long to call," I taunted.

"How dare you have Sebastian fire me."

"Why do you sound so surprised. When you leaked that story full of lies about Diamond and Cameron, all bets were off."

"I told you I had nothing to do with that."

"Save it, Darcy. I'm done playing with you. I know you get a sick pleasure screwing up other people's lives, but you fucked with the wrong girl this time. Having Sebastian fire your ass is only the beginning. Get ready, Darcy 'cause you goin' all the way down."

"If you think I'm going to be brought down by the likes of you, Kennedy, you are sadly mistaken. You want to battle with me, get ready. This ain't my first time at the rodeo and it won't be my last so watch your back."

After Darcy ended the call I went right back to what I was doing. If I hadn't worked with her for all those years, I might've been a tad shaken by Darcy's threats. But once you've gotten down in the mud with pigs, you're never afraid to get dirty.

Blair

"Blair, he's perfect." Diamond beamed, as she held my newborn son.

"How long were you in labor?" Kennedy asked.

"Not long at all. It happened so fast. I was on my way to do the doctor for my weekly check up and my water broke. Next thing you know, I'm in the hospital pushing and a couple of hours later I'm holding my son."

"Girl, you got all the luck. I was in labor for over 15 hours with Destiny. I told the doctor if they didn't get her out of me in the next five minutes I was going to rip her out myself."

"I remember that. You were so tired from pushing Destiny out you didn't even feel like holding her," I said, recalling that day perfectly.

"I was so damn weak, but once I did hold my baby I never wanted to let her go. Destiny was my little angel."

"That's how I feel about my son," I said, reaching my arms out so Diamond could give him back to me.

"Did you let Kirk know you had the baby?" Kennedy inquired.

"Yeah, I sent him a text letting him know I had the baby and what hospital we were at, but I doubt he'll show up because he didn't respond."

"I think you spoke too soon," Diamond said when Kirk walked through the door. I started to smile until the same woman I saw him with at the restaurant a few weeks ago, walked in right behind him.

"Oh no, he didn't," Diamond spit, rising up from her chair. "Did you really bring some chick up in this hospital room with you to see your son. Oh hell no!"

"I'm not some chick. I'm his girlfriend," the woman said, looking like she was dressed to hit the club instead of visiting the maternity ward at the hospital.

"I'm not talking to you," Diamond popped, twisting her neck all the way around to face Kirk's girlfriend. "As a matter of fact, you need to get yo' ass out this hospital room before I throw you out."

"Diamond, calm down," I said, wanting to keep the peace.

"Calm down my ass! This disrespectful simple nigga wanna stroll up in here with this dummy," Diamond said, pointing her finger at Kirk's girl, "bringing his negativity. You might as well not have even shown up."

"I don't want any problems. I just came to see my son. Tonya was with me when I got the text so I brought her too."

Kennedy and Diamond both stood there shaking their heads.

"Do you really hate me that much?"

"What are you talkin' 'bout, Blair?" Kirk asked as if he was clueless to what I was saying.

"This is the happiest day of my life. I gave birth to

our son. Why would you purposely ruin it by bringing her? She could've stayed in the car or even in the waiting room out there," I said, pointing towards the door. "For you to have her in my room where I'm celebrating bringing a healthy baby into this world with my friends who love me is cruel. So again I ask, do you really hate me that much?"

There was dead silence in the room as if everyone was waiting to hear Kirk's answer to my question. But there wouldn't be one. "I just want to hold my son, then I'll leave."

I looked down at my sweet baby who was sleeping so peacefully and then I gently lifted him up, handing him to his father.

"You better than me, I wouldn't let him hold nothing," I heard Diamond say.

"You ain't lying," Kennedy cosigned.

"Thank you," Kirk said, handing our son back to me after holding him for about five minutes. "Have you named him yet?"

"Not yet."

"I want him to have my last name."

"That's fine."

"I'll be in touch to make arrangements to see him again."

"Okay."

I was worried Diamond would trip Kirk when he walked past her on his way out the door, but she held it together. It didn't stop her or Kennedy from giving him the look of death.

"The balls on that man is something else," Kennedy said. "You handled that very well. Are you okay?"

"Not really, but I will be."

'That nigga is in love with you. I'm telling you. Only a hurt motherfucker in love, but too prideful to admit it, do some dumb shit like that."

"I think I'm gonna have to agree with Diamond on that. It's like Kirk's screaming for your attention, but instead of just asking for it, he rather hurt you so you'll react. It's still messed up."

"Damn straight, it's messed up. I wouldn't have let him hold my baby, bringing that silly broad up in my room. You is better than me fo' real," Diamond said, still heated.

"Kirk does continue to hurt me, but I don't want to keep our son from him. They deserve to have a relationship that's separate from us. I don't want to start his life with him in the middle of our problems. All this little boy wants is love and if Kirk wants to give that to him, I won't stand in the way."

"Whatever you decide to do, we support you one hundred percent," Kennedy stated. "So have you decided what you're going to name this handsome fella?"

"Donovan," I announced proudly. "It means dark warrior."

"Perfect." Diamond smiled, giving a thumbs up.

"I love it too, so Donovan it is."

"Donovan it is," we all said in unison.

Diamond

"Baby girl, I'm so glad you came over."

"Ma, I just saw you a few days ago when I dropped Destiny off," I said, sitting down on the living room couch.

"True, but I saw you for all of 30 seconds. The last few weeks you just come and go so quick. If I didn't know better, I would think you were running from me," my mother said with a frown.

"Oh please. I'm not running from you," I replied, nervously twisting in my seat.

"Are you sure?" my mom asked with a raised eyebrow. "I've been hearing about this so called baby Cameron has on the way with another woman. Is it true?"

I let out a deep sigh and put my head down. "I really don't want to talk about this," I huffed.

"So I take it that it is true then," my mom smacked, folding her arms. "So what you gon' do?"

"I don't know. We're not even sure it's his baby although Cameron thinks it is."

"That means he knows he was having unprotected sex with this woman probably more than once," she said, shaking her head. "That's some triflin' shit," my mom continued, never being one to bite her tongue.

"Don't you think I know this?" I snapped, becoming irritated.

"Since you know it, then like I said, what you gon' do? You need to leave his ass. I didn't raise you to be no doormat for a man. You let Rico take you for a ride, don't let Cameron do the same thing."

"I can't believe you are putting Rico and Cameron in the same category. Yes, what Cameron did is messed up, but Rico treated me like the bottom of his shoe and thought nothing of it. They are nothing alike. I thought you liked Cameron?" I said, shocked that my mom was telling me to leave my husband.

"I don't like nobody that doesn't treat my baby girl right. You have been nothing but good to that man and for him to cross you like this is unacceptable."

"Ma, I haven't been exactly perfect in this marriage either."

"What do mean? Did you cheat on Cameron too?"

"No, I didn't cheat on him, but he cheated when we were having serious problems."

"That was nothing. You told me you all had just had a little disagreement."

"I lied," I admitted. "I downplayed the severity of the situation. Cameron was considering divorce, but I was determined to save my marriage, so I didn't tell you how bad it was."

"Diamond, I hate that you felt the need to lie to me. But baby, what could you have done so bad that Cameron would want a divorce?"

"It's complicated. But he forgave me."

"So what you feel like you should forgive him too? Knowing your husband had sex with another woman is already a hard pill to swallow, but the possibility that a baby was conceived out of that cheating is a whole 'nother monster."

"I know... I know," I said solemnly.

"Remember, that's why I left your daddy. A baby didn't even come out of his creeping, but I couldn't get past his cheating. I got disgusted every time I saw his face," my mother said, as if the anger she harbored was still fresh in her mind.

"I hear what you're saying, but I haven't stopped loving Cameron. At the same time, I can't deny that I am torn. The idea of him having a baby with another woman and them being connected for the rest of their lives makes me wanna cry." Right after I divulged that, I could feel the tears swelling up in my eyes. I began coughing nervously, not in the mood to have a breakdown in my mother's living room.

"Diamond, it will be okay," my mother said, walking towards me with a box of tissues in her hand. "Nobody said being married was easy. No matter what you decide, you have my full support."

"I really do appreciate that, Ma," I said, taking some tissue and wiping the tears away. "Right about now, I need all the support I can get."

When I left my mother's house, I was so distraught thinking about the state of my marriage, that at first I didn't notice the nondescript Honda Accord behind me. I realized that the car had been following me from the time

I left my mother's crib. It could've been a coincidence, but for some reason I didn't think it was. I decided to make a quick turn on the next street, and when the Honda turned too, I knew my suspicions were correct.

"Who the fuck is you!" I popped loudly, glancing in my rearview mirror, trying to get a good look at the driver. But with the distance the person was keeping and the tint, which even covered half of the front window, I couldn't see shit. I wanted to slam on my breaks, so the driver could hit the back of my truck, giving me time to jump out and bum rush them. The problem with that was since I gave up the street life, I no longer kept protection on me. I felt it wasn't necessary being that I was the wife of an NBA player. My daily life was pretty simple. Clearly, I made a mistake.

I pressed down on the gas, picking up speed, trying to shake the driver, but they stayed on my ass. "This motherfucker is really trying me right now," I spit, making another quick left down a one-way street. After making two more turns, I looked back and I had finally lost them. "Yes!" I grinned, pumping my fist.

My excitement quickly disappeared when I realized whoever that was following me knew where my mother lived. "Who the hell is after me?" I asked myself out loud. "And how do they know where my mother lives... would they hurt her?" The questions began flooding my mind and paranoia kicked in. I fidgeted around the passenger seat looking for my cell phone, desperately wanting to call my mother. But before I could warn her, I heard a loud crash, and my body jerked forward. I had jumped a curb and in the process smashed into the back of a parked car. Right when I was putting my car in reverse, I noticed the tinted Honda Accord slowly coming down the street.

Kennedy

"Good morning, gorgeous," Sebastian said, standing over me, holding my favorite smoothie. "It's time to get up."

"I seriously doubt I look gorgeous right now," I said, sitting up in the bed, reaching for the drink. "This is exactly what I need. A few sips of this and I'll have more than enough energy to get out of bed."

"You think you'll have enough energy for something else too," Sebastian said, bending down next to me and nuzzling my neck.

"Oh definitely." I smiled, admiring every muscle on his chest. "Being next to me like this with no shirt on is giving me the easy access I like," I teased.

"Really now," Sebastian said, as his nuzzling turned into wet kisses. His kisses continued down my neck to my breast. When he got to my nipple his soft lips sucked them delicately. I closed my eyes feeling warm inside, as my nipples were my hot spot. Then in an instant Sebastian stopped cold.

"Why did you stop?" I questioned, ready to get it in.

"I'm running late for a meeting. I should've left 15 minutes ago."

"So why did you get me all worked up, when you knew you had to go?"

"Just wanted you to know what you had to look forward to after the party tonight." He smiled.

"You're such an asshole." I laughed, smacking Sebastian with a pillow.

"Maybe, but I'm your asshole," he said, kissing me on the lips. Don't forget I'll be back to pick you up at seven."

"I know. You've been reminding me since I got to LA."

"I can't help that I'm ready to show off my girlfriend." He smiled before disappearing in the bathroom.

Sebastian's declaration put a schoolgirl smile across my face. I slithered under the cover, tightly holding a pillow to my face, as I continued to smile, filled with happiness. It felt like we were back in college, falling in love all over again. This time would be different though. I had no plans of messing it up.

I fell asleep for a few hours before waking back up. I was feeling a little lazy, but it was time for me to start getting ready for Sebastian's party. I was wearing a custom Michael Costello sequin mini dress with sheer detailing throughout and on the sides. I decided to pair it with some sky-high black pumps that would have my man salivating.

I took my time in the shower, enjoying the hot water cascading down my body. There was a sense of peace surrounding me and it felt so good. The reason for my new found serenity was Sebastian. Everything felt so right when we were together and that's why tonight

I was prepared to tell Sebastian I would move to LA and live with him. I was ready to start my new life with him and I was excited about sharing the news.

By the time I finally finished taking my shower I had to hurry up and get dressed because Sebastian would be here to pick me up soon. Once I slithered into the mini dress, it seemed to fit even better than before. "Sebastian is going to have a hard on for me all night with this on," I said doing a quick twirl in the full-length mirror. I opted for a nude lip and my hair in an up do to complete my look.

While securing my bun, I heard a text message come through on my phone. At first I ignored it, but then I realized instead of calling, Sebastian might be texting to let me know he was here. I dabbled on a little clear lipgloss over my nude lipstick before reaching for my phone.

"It is my baby." I smiled when I saw his name. "There's an attachment. I wonder what he sent me," I continued talking out loud as I slipped on my black pumps.

Within an instant my smile shifted to a frown when I opened the attachment. "This picture has to be from today," I said, noticing the clothes he had on before he left was laying on the bed.

There Sebastian was in bed naked, asleep next to some woman who was also naked. *This motherfucker left me to go fuck the next chick and got caught out there. The chick obviously knows about me and put his cheating ass on blast. Damn Sebastian and I thought what we had was special. I wish I would've stayed thinking you were dead*, I thought to myself as I sat on the bed crying my heart out.

Blair

"Good morning, Donovan," I said, taking him out of his crib. It seemed like yesterday he was born and now he was three months old. Each day I spent with him, I not only discovered new things about my son, but I also learned so much about myself. The entire experience was simply amazing.

"Are you ready for us to go for our morning walk," I said, tickling him underneath his chubby chin. What had now become our daily ritual of me pushing Donovan through Central Park, had literally made every pregnancy pound I gained vanish.

After I got Donovan situated in his stroller, we headed out. "It's time to go," I said, opening the front door only to find Skee standing there. "Skee, what are you doing here?"

"I know I shouldn't have popped up like this, but you've been on my mind and so has he," he said, staring down at Donovan. "Wow, what a cute baby."

"You say that like you're surprised."

"I'm not around many kids and the babies I have

seen aren't really that cute to me so I guess I am surprised that he's so cute."

"Skee, you have no filter whatsoever."

"What can I say, I was born like that."

"I appreciate you coming to check on me, but we're actually headed out for our morning walk through Central Park."

"Nice. I guess that's how you got your figure back already."

"It is. I never knew walking would be so great for my body, mind, and spirit."

"Do you mind if I join you?"

"You want to go walking with us?"

"Yeah, why not. I got on the right shoes."

"You're not worried about people stopping you and wanting an autograph?"

"We're going for a walk through Central Park, nobody will bother us."

"Then let's go."

"Blair, I don't think I ever told you this but I'm sorry for all the BS I put you through. I should've treated you better when I had you."

"Where is all this coming from?"

"Ever since we got back the results of the paternity test and I found out the child wasn't mine, I haven't stopped thinking about what could've been. If I hadn't messed up we could've been pushing our baby through the park right now."

"Thank you for telling me that, but going through this pregnancy and having Donovan, I've learned that you can't let your emotions get weighed down by having regrets. You live and hopefully you'll learn so that every new journey becomes better. I'm a better person because of you."

"How are things between you and Kirk?" Skee asked.

"It started off really bad, but it's becoming somewhat decent. But even dealing with Kirk has made me a better person."

"You seem to be in a good place."

"I am. This is the happiest I've ever been in my life. I don't think I understood the true meaning of unconditional love until Donovan came into my life."

"I'm happy for you, Blair. Seeing you like this makes me fall in love with you all over again."

"Skee, our relationship didn't work before and I doubt it would work now."

"I know your focus is on spending time with your son and it should be. I'm not trying to complicate things by having you jump into another relationship with me. What I would like is if we could go back to building our friendship. I genuinely care about you, Blair."

"I would like that. It was always so easy for me to open up and discuss things with you, no matter how painful. Diamond is dealing with her own issues right now and Kennedy, who I never thought would find love, is in a full-fledged relationship, so neither one of them have much time for me right now."

"I can be that friend you pour your heart out to."

"You sure about that?"

"Yes, and we can start this new friendship by you telling me why Kirk hasn't moved you and his son to a nicer and more secure building?"

"I love our apartment. It's a sublease but for now it works."

"That's not answering my question, Blair. Is he even paying child support?"

"Yes, he is and a very generous amount, but I have to live within my means. You know how expensive living in New York is. Kirk isn't my man so I can only expect for him to help take care of our son, not me."

"Fuck that. You not some random chick he knocked up. Plus, that nigga rich and whether you all are together or not, you're the mother of his child. He should want the both of you to live good."

"Kirk doesn't see it that way. I can't blame him. He was hurt that I didn't tell him what happened between us. He thought I was trying to trick him and put the baby off on him. Which wasn't true, but I did handle things all wrong. Now I guess you can say I'm paying the price."

"But the baby is his so whatever happened in the past needs to be left there."

"I agree, but Donovan and I are better than great. Pretty soon I'll be back to work and the money will start rolling in. Once that happens then I'll upgrade to a nicer place that I can afford."

"You're the best, Blair. Donovan is lucky to have you for his mother."

"Thanks, but I'm the lucky one," I said, looking down at my watch. "Can you believe we've been walking for over an hour already. But we're almost back to my place. Are you holding up alright?" I asked Skee.

"I got this. This walk was what I needed though. I can understand why you do it everyday. It's relaxing."

"Very. Do you want to come back upstairs? I always make a smoothie after my walk."

"Sounds good, smoothie it is."

Skee and I were talking, giggling, and laughing like old times as we headed back to my apartment. It felt nice to be spending time with someone I felt so comfortable with. I was having so much fun getting to know my new baby that I hadn't realized how much I missed adult companionship.

"Enough of the jokes, Skee, I'm tired of laughing," I cracked as I playfully punched him.

"What the hell is going on?" the loud deep voice coming down the hall startled me until I looked up and saw Kirk standing outside my apartment door.

"Kirk, what are you doing here?"

"I came to see my son."

"You should've called and let me know you were coming."

"Why in the hell do you have him around my son?"

"Skee is a friend of mine who decided to go for a walk with us."

"I don't want him around my son."

"Man, you need to chill," Skee said, clearly feeling disrespected.

"This don't have nothing to do with you. That's my son. This is between me and Blair."

"Don't come at me like that," Skee said stepping forward.

"Both of you stop," I said, putting my hands up as if calling a truce. "Kirk, can you come back later on or maybe tomorrow?"

"Why should I have to leave? I came here to spend time with Donovan. If anybody should go it should be that mothefucker."

"You got one more motherfuckin' time to..."

"Skee, please ignore him. You all should not be doing this in front of the baby. Skee, I need to talk to Kirk alone. I'll call you later. Thanks for coming by. I really did enjoy spending time with you," I said, giving him a hug.

"So did I. Make sure you call me."

"I will," I said before we went inside my apartment. After I closed the door, Kirk reached in the stroller to get Donovan who was sleeping.

"I don't want Skee around my son... ever."

"You have no right to tell me that. Skee isn't dangerous or harmful to our son."

"You know how I feel about him."

"This is coming from the same man that brought his girlfriend to my hospital room right after I had my baby. I will never keep you from your son, but you can't tell me who I can have around Donovan."

"Are you seeing him?"

"Huh?"

"Are you seeing Skee again?"

"If I am, it's none of your business."

"He's no good for you, but yet you always let him back into your life."

"I know you're not the forgiving type, but people do change. Skee isn't perfect, but neither am I, nor you for that matter."

"I have to go to practice, but I'll be back to see Donovan when I'm done. We also have some unfinished business to discuss because this conversation isn't over."

I shook my head in frustration once Kirk slammed the door behind him. His attitude regarding Skee was beyond petty. If Kirk thought for one second I would allow him to regulate my personal life he was in for a rude awakening.

Diamond

"Fuckin' drive!" I screamed, banging my fist on the steering wheel when I couldn't get my car to start. I kept pressing down on the gas and pressing the start button, but got nothing. I looked out the rearview mirror and saw the nondescript Honda that had been following me, slowly coming towards me. After a few seconds it just stopped.

I reached over and grabbed my cell phone. My heart started pounding when I realized I had less than 5 percent battery life left. I had to call my mother and make sure she was okay. I wasn't sure if the person following me had a partner and if they were waiting outside my mother's house or worse, had already gotten to her. I couldn't take that chance. First, I dialed her cell phone and it rang several times then went to voicemail. I then tried the home phone and her answering machine came on.

"Answer the damn phone!" I yelled at my iPhone. Finally on the fourth or fifth try, we connected.

"Hey Diamond, what...."

"Thank God you answered. Are you okay?" I asked, cutting my mother off.

"I'm fine. You just left here. Besides me being pissed at your husband, didn't I seem okay to you... and why do you sound like that? You breathing all hard, did something happen?"

"I was calling you nonstop and you didn't answer your phone."

"I was using the bathroom. Is everything okay? You don't sound right," my mother said in a concerned tone.

"Listen, I don't have long to talk because my phone is about to die. But make sure you keep the door locked and don't open it for anybody you don't know. If you see someone parked outside that seems suspicious to you call the police."

"Diamond, what the hell is going on? Are you in some sort of trouble?" she asked, becoming panicked. "Tell me baby girl. I keep a gun and I will use it."

While my mother was talking I kept trying to start my car and getting the same results. I looked in the rearview mirror and noticed the front door of the Honda open slowly. I couldn't see who was getting out, but whoever it was I knew they were coming for me. I glanced up to see the exact street I was on so I could tell my mother to send some help.

"Ma, I need you to call the police. I'm on...." Before I could get out another word my phone was dead. A rush of despair hit me like a punch to the chest. I felt in my gut, nothing good was going to come of this. At that moment I had to decide what to do next. Staying in the car with the doors locked wasn't an option for me because windows can be broken. I had to get out and make a run for it.

Although this wasn't a busy street, I was hoping I could find someone to stop and help me. I grabbed my purse and right when I hopped out the car and was about to take off running, I was stopped dead in my tracks.

"Lela, you don't want to do this," I said calmly although I had never felt this level of fear in my life. Not even when Parrish robbed or kidnapped me. I think it's because I knew he was being motivated by money or I felt I could out slick him. Staring at Lela, her eyes were empty. All she wanted was me dead. "Whatever's going on with you, we can talk about it. So you can put the gun down," I said, trying to reason with her."

She did this wicked, eerie laugh before speaking. "Even with a gun pointed at your head, you want to stand there all calm, cool and collected. You really are a piece of work, Diamond. But your time is up. We have nothing to talk about, unless you want to make a plea for me to shoot you in the heart instead of the face so your family can give you an open casket. But then again, you have no heart."

"Lela, I know you blame me for what happened to Rico, but it's not true. Killing me isn't going to bring him back and I know you don't want to spend the rest of your life in jail."

"You think I give a damn about going to jail! Not only did you take Rico from me I know you're responsible for my brother being killed too! You evil whore!"

"What are you talking about? I didn't even know you had a brother," I lied, trying my best to save my life.

"Shut up! I'm so sick of your lies! The man that you hired to follow and scare me admitted it right before I blew his brains out last night."

"I have no idea what you're talking about. I never hired any man to follow you. This is clearly a huge misunderstanding," I stuttered, swallowing hard.

"The only misunderstanding is with those fuckin' cops that never charged you with killing Rico. If you had went to jail for that then my brother would be alive right now. But like the snake you are, you slithered your way out of that, but your nine lives are finally up. Bitch, you 'bout to die," Lela spit with venom. I closed my eyes and all I could think about was my mom having to bury her daughter and Destiny growing up without a mother.

"Lela," I said, opening my eyes back up. "I know you're hurting, but think about Rico's daughter. Do you really want Destiny to grow up without her mother?" I said, as I continued grasping for straws, praying something would snap Lela out of her killer mode.

"Save it, Diamond. Destiny will be better off without a trifling mother like you. She'll have her grandparents to raise her."

My body began shaking as it became more and more clear that I wouldn't be able to talk my way out of this. Lela had made up her mind that she was going to kill me and there was nothing I could do about it. I closed my eyes again and began praying. I was begging God to save me. I had made some questionable decisions in my life and definitely was no saint, but I didn't want it to end like this. I was praying so hard and when I heard police sirens in the distance, and the sound began to get closer I just knew my prayers had been answered.

Somebody finally saw this crazy woman pointing a gun at me and called the police. Praise The Lord... save me Jesus, I thought to myself, as my trembling body began to ease up knowing help was on the way. Within a couple minutes several police cars were surrounding us and officers were positioned with their weapons at Lela.

"Put down your gun and raise your hands now!" an officer directed over a bullhorn.

"Lela, it's over. Do what the police say so you don't get hurt."

"Do you think I care about getting hurt? I'm already dead," she said with a sinister smile across her face. Without saying another word she pulled the trigger. Before I felt the hot lead ripping through my chest, I saw the police unleash their ammunition on Lela, riddling her body with bullets. We hit the pavement at the same time as our blood flowed and it was lights out for both of us.

Kennedy

On my flight back to New York from LA, I kept looking at the photo of Sebastian sleeping naked next to some woman he had clearly fucked and decided to put his trifling ass on blast. I was so happy I was able to catch a last minute flight because although I could've stayed at a hotel, I couldn't stand being in LA any longer. The city only represented negativity to me now. I decided to turn my phone off because if I didn't I would stare at the photo for the duration of my flight.

"Are you going to tell me why you won't take Sebastian's calls?" Tammy questioned, as she sat some papers down on my desk.

"No," I said, flipping through the papers, never looking up.

"For the last week I've been telling him you're either in a meeting, or you just stepped out the office. I don't know how much longer I can take all his interrogating before I let it slip that you're simply ignoring his calls. Although, I think by now he's figured that out. I mean really, Kennedy, you're not going to be able to avoid Sebastian forever. At some—"

"Tammy, how long are you going to stand there and babble because I'm more than positive you have some work you need to be doing. As a matter of fact, where's Diamond? I told you to get her on the phone for me over an hour ago."

"I've been trying to reach her, but her phone keeps going straight to voicemail. Maybe she's decided to take a few days off. I mean she does have a lot going on."

"Keep trying," I said, dismissing Tammy so she would get out of my face. I decided to try Diamond myself again. She was going through a lot so Tammy could very well be right that she was taking a few days off, but I found it weird that she wasn't answering her phone or returning my texts. *Let me call Blair*, I thought to myself as her phone rang.

"Hey, girl, what's going on?" Blair answered.

"Is that Donovan I hear in the back crying?"

"Yes, I need to change his diaper. You know mommy duty don't stop, but I love it," Blair laughed.

"I know you do. I'm not going to keep you, but I was wondering have you heard from Diamond?"

"I got skills. I can change a diaper and talk to you at the same time. But ummm, I spoke to Diamond briefly a few days ago, but you know this baby situation has her in a real funk. When I called her, I could tell she really wasn't in the mood to talk so I've been giving her some space. I'm sure we'll hear from her soon. You know how Diamond can get, but she's strong so she'll be straight."

"Yeah, you're right. I'm sure she'll be back in the office doing her normal shit talking soon."

"Of course. I haven't had a chance to really talk to you since you got back from LA. How was your trip? I know you had fun catching up with Sebastian. Don't let me find out you was down there making a baby with him," Blair joked. "Kennedy..." she called out when I remained silent after what she said. "Are you there?"

"I'm here," I replied somberly.

"Are you okay?"

"No, but it's too much to say over the phone. Are you going to be busy later on?"

"No, why don't you stop by after you leave the office."

"I need someone to talk to so that would be nice. Plus, I can see that cute baby of yours."

"Sounds like a plan!"

"I'll call you when I'm on the way."

"Cool, see you soon," Blair said before hanging up the phone.

I put my head down and I really wanted to break down and cry, but felt that would be way too unprofessional. I was a boss and the last thing I wanted my employees to see was me crying at work over my man, or better yet my ex-man. I had completely cut Sebastian off without uttering one single word to him. I felt I didn't need to. He knew what the fuck he did and he could figure the shit out for himself.

"What is it now?" I said to Tammy when she came strolling back over to my desk.

"I thought you would want to see this," she said, tossing down the New York Post. "I meant to give it to you earlier, but you didn't seem to be in the mood to entertain bogus gossip."

I gave Tammy a side eye at her sarcastic remark before opening the paper. "If this is some more bullshit about Cameron and the baby I see why Diamond been missing."

"Go to Page Six. They're featuring both of your girls today," Tammy informed me.

"Diamond and Blair?" I questioned, flipping the pages.

"Yep," Tammy said as soon as I turned to the page.

"Wow, this nonsense never stops," I said shaking my head in disgust. "NBA Superstar Cameron Robinson's lovechild due any day," I read the article headline out loud. "No wonder we can't get in touch with Diamond. She's probably somewhere plotting the murder of Cameron and this hussy," I continued as I looked at the girl's picture. She was cheesing extra hard.

"I guess this means she's Darcy client again," Tammy said.

"I doubt she ever stopped being her client. I don't know which one of them is messier."

"Well it gets even messier. Check out the tea they think they're spilling about Blair."

"What the fuck! Where do they come up with this mess!" I gasped.

"Do you think Blair knows?" Tammy questioned

"No. I just spoke to her. If she knew anything she would've said something.

"If I didn't know better I would think there was some sort of conspiracy to drive me, Blair, and Diamond crazy. Can we just get one day with no drama, damn!" I huffed grabbing my purse.

"Where are you going?" Tammy wanted to know as I headed for the door.

"I have to get out of this office. I'm taking the rest of the day off. I'll see you tomorrow. If a client emergency comes up, don't call me. You deal with it. Bye!" I said, not looking back.

Blair

"Kirk, what are you doing here?' I said after opening my front door. His new habit of just popping up was beginning to work my last nerve. I wanted things to be cordial between us, but this had to stop.

"I need to talk to you," he said, bypassing me as he walked in the apartment like he lived there too.

"We can talk, but coming over without calling in advance has to stop. I can't come to your crib unannounced, so what makes you think it's acceptable for you to do it?" I said, closing the door.

"Why should it be a problem for you unless you have company you don't want me to know about? Somebody like Skee, maybe?"

"You can't be serious. I already told you my position regarding Skee and it hasn't changed. My personal relationships are none of your business and vice versa."

"It is my business when everybody running around here thinking my son is his!" Kirk yelled.

"Keep your voice down. I just put Donovan down for a nap," I said, walking over to his bedroom to check on him before closing the door. "Now what are you rambling on about?"

"So you haven't seen today's paper?" Kirk asked, holding up what looked to be the *New York Post.*

"When you're taking care of a baby all day, reading the newspaper is nowhere on your to do list."

"Well maybe you need to incorporate it in there, especially if you're going to have my son around your ex. Or are you guys back together?"

"No, we're not, but again, it's none of your business," I said taking the paper from Kirk to see what had him all hot and bothered. "This picture was taken when we came back from that walk and you were here. You know how these gossip columns are."

"The headline says that they finally know who the father of model/actress Blair's baby is. Rap Superstar Skee Patron!" he screamed.

"I can read and didn't I tell you to keep your voice down or don't you care about waking Donovan," I snapped.

"You don't care that people think the father of our son is Skee?"

"No, because we know it's not true. We can't control what some newspaper prints. It's meaningless gossip."

"You need to have yo' girl Kennedy make them write a retraction."

"Kirk, once you start responding to gossip you have to keep responding. Just ignore it and it will go away. They'll be on the next story next week."

"This ain't some story. They talkin' 'bout my son and if you won't handle it then I will," he said before leaving abruptly, slamming the door.

Kirk had me so riled up I wanted a drink, but since I was still breastfeeding, I opted against it. I decided to sit down and try to relax, but before I could even get comfortable, I heard a knock at the door. *What the fuck does Kirk want now? I don't feel like hearing no more of his shit,* I thought to myself while going to open the door.

"What is it?" I huffed. "Kennedy, hi! Sorry, I thought you were someone else."

"Let me guess... Kirk. I saw him leaving when I was on my way in."

"Did he see you?"

"No. He was already getting in his car. He seemed a little agitated. Would it have anything to do with the write up in the *Post* today?" Kennedy asked, sitting down.

"I guess everyone saw it, but me," I said, taking a seat across from Kennedy. "Kirk was so livid. He actually told me to have you contact the *Post* and have them write a retraction."

"I can put in a call and make that happen."

"Thank you, but no thanks. I don't want the spotlight on Donovan. Like I told Kirk, this story will die and they'll be on to the next lie."

"True, but it must be eating Kirk up that they think his son is Skee's. You all did look cozy in that picture. Are you back seeing Skee?" Kennedy questioned.

"No. He came to see me when I was about to take Donovan for a walk. It was completely innocent. I didn't even know someone took our picture. Kirk doesn't even want Skee around our son."

"I bet!"

"Yeah, but he has no right to tell me who can be around our son. I mean, do you think I really want that chick he brought to the hospital playing mommy to Donovan? But I'm not going to be one of those women telling my baby father he can't have his girlfriend around our child," I said.

"I feel you, but I doubt Kirk is going to be as understanding. Whether he wants to admit it or not he still has feelings for you and I'm sure he doesn't want Skee or any other man around his son or you."

"Whatever. I'm over talking about Kirk," I said, throwing up my hand.

"I feel you. But since you didn't see the article about you and Skee I guess you didn't see the write up about Cameron's lovechild being due any day now?"

"What! That was in the paper too? Sheesh, poor Diamond."

"I know. Now I get why she's MIA. They haven't even had time to enjoy being married without dealing with bullshit. I don't know how much one marriage can take," Kennedy said.

"So true, but I'm still cheering for them. I know how much they love each other. Let's keep our fingers crossed that love will be enough to get them through this storm. Okay, now that we've covered me and Diamond, let's get to you."

"Before I start running off at the mouth let me see that sweet baby," Kennedy said, grinning from ear to ear.

"Girl, Donovan is knocked out and we are not about to wake him up. You might have to see him on your next visit. Now proceed," I said, leaning back in my seat. "I want to know what happened on your trip to LA."

"I'll let you see for yourself," Kennedy said, handing me her phone.

"Is that Sebastian in bed with another woman," I stated in shock.

"That's exactly what it is. "

"How did you get this picture?"

"It was sent from his phone so I'm assuming the woman sent it to me to put his cheating ass on blast."

"Boy oh boy, these men always get caught slipping and it be the slut they cheating with that makes sure they get caught. When will they learn to keep it in their pants," I said, shaking my head. "I'm so sorry, Kennedy."

"Not as sorry as I am. I felt like I got another shot at love when he came back in my life but instead he broke my heart."

"What did he say when you confronted him about the picture?" I wanted to know.

"Nothing."

"What you mean nothing? His dumbass didn't give you any sort of explanation."

"Nope, because I didn't ask for one. His no good ass know what the fuck he did," Kennedy shot back with an attitude.

"Wait a minute. You're confusing me. Are you saying you haven't told Sebastian that some thirsty side chick sent you a naked picture of him in bed?"

"That's exactly what I'm saying," Kennedy retorted.

"Kennedy, you can't let Sebastian off that easy. You need to confront him over his foul behavior and let him know that he hurt you."

"Why? So he can get the last laugh and I can feel like an even bigger fool for falling for his lies."

"You're not a fool. The only fool in this equation is Sebastian and the silly ho that sent you the photo. You believed in this man. At this point, it's not about him; you deserve to get some closure. Right now you're angry and rightfully so, but if you leave things the way they are, you'll harbor nothing but resentment. One day you will meet the right man and you don't need to bring that negative baggage with you, trust me," I said, reflecting on my own relationships.

"You're right, but I don't want Sebastian to know how badly he's hurt me. He already took my heart should he take my pride too," Kennedy said, tearing up.

"I know you're used to being in control and having everything together, but it doesn't make you any less of a strong woman because you allowed yourself to be vulnerable to a man you loved."

"You're right, but it doesn't make me feel any better."

"After you curse Sebastian's ass out and officially dump him, I promise you will feel a whole lot better," I said. "Did you just smile?" I laughed, patting Kennedy's leg.

"Yep, I did. Thanks for the advice because not only was it needed, but I'm going to use it."

"You're going to call Sebastian?"

"Sure am, later on tonight when I get home and I'm settled in," Kennedy said, nodding her head.

"I don't care what time it is, you better call and tell me in detail what you said and his response," I said, reaching for my cell phone. "I'm not done yet... just one second let me get this call," I continued, putting up my finger. "Hello."

"Hi Blair, this is Diamond's mother."

"Hi Ms. O'Toole, how are you?"

"Not good. Not good at all," she said. I could hear

that she was choking up, as if trying not to cry.

"What's wrong... did something happen to Diamond?"

"Yes, she was shot. I'm at the hospital. She's in surgery right now."

"Oh my gosh! I'm on the way!" I screamed out in a panicked voice before quickly ending the call.

"What happened?" Kennedy stood up and asked. Her face drenched in fear.

"Diamond has been shot. She's in surgery right now. Fuck! I was so anxious to get there that I forgot to ask her mother what hospital she's at."

"Calm down, Blair. In my gut I felt something was wrong, but nothing like this."

"I'm going to call her mother back and find out what hospital Diamond's at. You go 'head and go and I'll text you the information. I need to call the babysitter. I'll meet you at the hospital as soon as she gets here." My hands were shaking so badly I could barely press the buttons on my cell phone.

"Blair, try to relax. You said yourself how strong Diamond is. She'll be fine. I'll call you as soon as I get to the hospital and give you an update," Kennedy said.

"Okay, I'll be there soon." Kennedy gave me a hug trying to console me before she left, but I wouldn't be able to relax until I knew what condition Diamond was in. I was praying that it wasn't too serious, but I had a bad feeling it was much much worse.

Diamond

My body was paralyzed as if I was frozen. I didn't know what the hell was wrong with me. The last thing I remembered was Lela pointing a gun at me, pulling the trigger and then the cops shooting her. After that my mind was completely blank. *Oh NO! Am I dead! Did Lela kill me? Is this what happens when you go to the other side?* I yelled, but no words were coming out and my mouth wasn't moving.

Then I heard sounds and movement around me. At first, it seemed like jumbled noise, but then it was like my hearing became clear.

"We were able to remove the bullet that was lodged near her heart, but she lost a lot of blood. Your wife is in a coma and the next 24 to 48 hours are critical. Right now all we can do is wait."

'Thank you, doctor."

"My daughter can't die... she just can't," I heard my mother cry out.

"Ms. O'Toole, would you mind if I have a moment alone with my wife?" I heard Cameron ask.

"Okay, I'll be right outside."

So I'm not dead, I'm in a coma. There's still hope. But damn, does that mean I'm going to come out the coma and if so, when. I wanted to believe all would be right in the world, but this not being able to move thing was really fucking with me. Damn that Lela. I began feeling like I was drifting off. I wasn't sure if I was trying to sleep or if that meant I was dying. I wanted to stay awake and when I heard the sound of Cameron's voice, it gave me the willpower to do just that.

"I would give anything to trade places with you right now. That's how much I love you Diamond. I don't want you to go for my own selfish reasons, but the main reason I rather it be me than you lying in this hospital bed is because of Destiny. When I met you and saw how much you adored her, it made me fall in love with you even more. I knew if I could just get a small piece of that amount of love from you, it would be more than enough to get us through anything."

Listening to those words Cameron said were the sweetest I ever heard. I wanted to reach out my hand and touch him, but my body seemed to still be frozen. Then I wanted to cry, but not one tear would fall.

"I know you've been through a lot these last few months and I take all the blame. This baby situation has me so stressed, but instead of me being worried about my feelings, I should've tried harder to comfort you. I was selfish and I'm sorry. I hate that I'm saying all this when you can't even hear me, but I have so much guilt inside and if I don't let it out I'ma die inside," Cameron cried.

It broke my heart that Cameron was in pain. For these last few months part of me didn't think our marriage would survive, but I never stopped loving him although I wondered if he still loved me too. Now I knew that he did, but at this point, it might not even matter.

"Baby, you can't die. You can't leave our family and me. We have so much more to do together. You're everything to me. I can't even imagine my life without you in it. Dear God, I'm begging you to please bring my wife back to me."

I wanted to scream at the top of my lungs that I wanted to come back too. I wanted to be with Destiny, my mother, and with all that was going on in our marriage I wanted to be with Cameron too. If only I could speak. In my head, I could talk, but when I would try to move my mouth, no words would come out. This seemed like it was worse than actually being dead. I felt like a prisoner in my own body.

"Cameron, I apologize if I'm interrupting, but I really would like a moment to spend some time alone with my daughter."

"Of course, Ms. O'Toole. Would you like for me to go pick up Destiny?"

"Yes, but please let me be the one to tell her about Diamond. I just think it would be better that way."

"I understand. I'll call you once I've picked her up," I heard Cameron say before leaving.

"My sweet, beautiful, Diamond. Girl, you gon' give yo' mama a heart attack. You know I can't bury you, you supposed to bury me first and chile I'm too tired to raise Destiny. That girl is a handful just like you." My mother laughed before she started crying. I wasn't sure how many more tears I could take.

"It seems like just a minute ago you were sitting

across from me in my living room, now you're laying in a hospital bed in a coma. What sort of trick is the universe playing on me? Whatever it is, I wish it would stop.

"Baby girl, I promise, I'm about to crawl in that bed with you, if you don't make it. You can't let that happen because then my precious grandbaby won't have a mother or a grandmother. We can't do that to Destiny. She doesn't deserve that. Plus, I don't think Cameron would make it without you either. You know I'm feeling some kinda way about him right now, but I can look into that man's eyes and tell that he truly loves you. There's no denying that. So I'm trying to be nice to him because I know that is what you would want." My mother giggled.

She was right, I would want her to be nice to Cameron because if I didn't make it and died, they would need to lean on each other to get through it. Destiny would need both of them too. It hurt my heart to even contemplate that I wouldn't pull through, but I had to accept there was a real possibility I would never come out of my coma or I might even die.

Kennedy

"How is she?" Blair asked, running up to me practically out of breath.

"I haven't had a chance to see Diamond yet, all I know is she's in a coma."

"A coma! Oh no," Blair said, sitting down in a chair as if she were trying to keep herself from passing out. "Where is Diamond's mother?"

"In the room with Diamond. I'm waiting for her to come out so I can go in."

"Which room? I have to see her," Blair said with tears rolling down her cheeks. I pointed towards the room and before I could say another word she took off.

I sat down and shook my head. I reflected back to the time we all believed that Diamond had been killed and how relieved we were when we found out she was alive. We all had a strong united front during that trying time, but this time felt different. If Diamond didn't come out her coma, I knew none of our lives would be the same.

It seemed like it took forever for Ms. O'Toole and Blair to come out of Diamond's room. Both were in tears and were too upset to talk. As they consoled each other I went in her room. On the inside, I was crying also, but I knew at least one of us had to be strong and decided that person would be me.

"Diamond, girl, you got everybody in an uproar. Now gone 'head and wake up so we can stop losing our minds over here," I said playfully. "If only it was that simple… right. But seriously, I'm not going to be in here all night talking your head off. You already know what's up. We have an empire to build. We can't do that if you're asleep. So wake up… please.

"You know I hate begging, but I need you—we all do. Poor Blair hasn't been able to walk straight or hold a full conversation since she found out you were in a coma." I laughed. "I know that's not funny, but you know how much Blair adores you and so do I. Plus, we haven't had our ladies-only vacation yet. I promise you, if you come out of this like the fighter I know you are, we're going to vacay for at least a week on a fabulous yacht. Now I know you're probably wondering where the hell I'm going to get this so called fabulous yacht from, but let me worry about that. I'm always up for a challenge and if making that happen can motivate you to open your eyes then baby it's a done deal." I smiled, kissing Diamond on her forehead. "I love you. Now get some rest. You're going to need it for all the plans I have for us."

The bright sunlight shining through my bedroom window woke me up early on a Saturday morning. I desperately wanted to sleep late, but lately that seemed impossible to do. The last two weeks seemed like the longest of my life. Diamond was still in a coma and the more time passed, the less likely it became that she would wake up. Before I had any more time to get caught up in the depressing thoughts that seemed to be greeting me each morning, I heard someone knocking on my front door. I lazily got out the bed not wanting to be bothered.

"Coming," I yelled out, putting on my bathrobe as the person continued knocking. "Yes?" I answered.

"It seems showing up at your front door is the only way I can have a conversation with you."

My initial reaction was to slam the door in Sebastian's face, but I knew we needed closure in our relationship. After talking with Blair, I had every intention of calling him, but after Diamond was shot, her situation had consumed just about all of my time and thoughts.

"Come in," I said coldly.

"I see you're not happy to see me. I guess it wasn't just my imagination that you were avoiding me. Do you want to tell me why?" Sebastian asked, sitting down on the couch.

I was rolling my eyes and calling him every name in the book as my back was turned away from him. I finally closed the door before facing him. I stood straight with my arms folded. I felt as if steam was coming out of my head, that's how pissed I was for Sebastian acting as if he didn't know why I couldn't stand his ass anymore. Or maybe he was unaware that his cover had been blown. For a second, I considered playing along with his pathetic game, but I scratched that idea out of my head quickly. I had no interest in entertaining his bullshit because the quicker I let him know what was up, the quicker I could get him out of my apartment and out of my life.

"Are you going to come sit down and talk to me or just stand there?" Sebastian questioned as if he was the one that had a right to be incensed.

"Am I detecting an attitude in your voice?"

"You damn right. You've basically had me in stalker mode for the last few weeks and I'm scratching my head trying to understand why. I leave to handle some business and I come back to pick you up so we can attend an event together, but you're gone. Yes, I was late and I should've called, but that would be some silly shit for you to shut me out over," Sebastian stated through clenched teeth.

"Do you care to explain why you were late... or no?" I asked calmly, curious to see what his comeback excuse would be.

"What does that have to do with anything?"

"It has to do with everything. Now are you going to tell me or not?" Sebastian put his head down and squeezed his hands together as if becoming angrier. "Did my question make you uncomfortable?" I mocked.

"Nah, it's just..." There was a long pause.

"It's just what?" I said, not backing down.

"I got held up," he finally said.

"Held up. That's a cute way of putting it. Why don't you give me the ugly way... you know, the truth."

"What the fuck do you mean the ugly way?"

"You know exactly what the fuck I mean! Stop sitting there like you don't know what the hell you did. You are so full of shit!" I spit, ready to pick up the vase on the end table and slam it across his head.

"Yo, what is wrong with you? Yes, I was really late. Shit happens, but you need to calm the fuck down."

"Shit happens like you being late because you're in some hotel room fucking some other chick?" I screamed, unable to contain how livid I was any longer.

"Fucking some other chick... Kennedy, you are seriously paranoid and delusional."

"Is that denial I hear coming out your mouth? The audacity," I spewed. "Delusional? Oh really. This is what you call delusional?" I yelled, as I headed towards my bedroom to retrieve my phone.

"Where are you going?" I heard Sebastian ask as I disappeared into my bedroom before returning with my phone in hand. I went to messages and scrolled to Sebastian's name.

"I'll ask again, is this what you call delusional?" I said, shoving my phone in Sebastian's face with the image of him butt naked asleep on the bed next to a naked woman. His eyes widened as he remained speechless. "Oh, now you have nothing to say. It's amazing when someone has receipts—it totally shuts the other person up."

"Where did you get this picture?"

"The chick you were fucking sent it to me from your phone. Don't you see your name big and bold at the top. Let me guess, you didn't know she caught you slipping. Well she did."

"This has to be some sort of crazy joke. This picture ain't even in my phone."

"The girl probably deleted the message after she sent it to me from your phone so you wouldn't know, dumbass. But it doesn't change the fact that it happened."

"That's not me," Sebastian said, shaking his head.

"What!"

"I mean it's me, but that never happened," he

mumbled. "You got that text from me the night I was late picking you up?"

"Yes, you idiot!" I barked.

"Can you stop with the name calling? I'm trying to figure this out."

"What is there to figure out? You left me at your crib and then went and fucked another woman and got busted. Now you know why I want nothing to do with you. And honestly, I have no desire to listen to you come up with lies to try and get out of this mess. So please just go."

"Kennedy, I had a meeting at the Belvedere restaurant in the Peninsula Hotel. The woman I was meeting with spilled some food on me and I did go upstairs to her room to clean up. We continued to talk business for a while up there and I did fall asleep. Originally, I didn't want to tell you that was the reason I was late because I knew it sounded somewhat suspicious and you might not believe me, but it's the truth."

"So that's your story and you're sticking to it?"

"Baby, it's the truth."

"Why would you fall asleep? It wasn't even late."

"I know, I was wondering the same thing. But when I woke up I was sitting in the chair and I fell out of it. Tiffany told me I just dozed off."

"Oh, so Tiffany is the woman in the pic your naked with?"

"Hell no!"

"Are you sure? I mean all you can see is the woman's body from the neck down."

"I know it's not Tiffany because she's not even the same complexion as the woman in the pic and I would remember if she had a tattoo like that on her wrist. Plus, why would Tiffany send you a picture like that. We were there discussing business. I've never had a sexual relationship with her."

I stood shaking my head completely thrown for a loop. I figured Sebastian would try and lie his way out of this, but never did I think this would be his excuse. It sounded absolutely preposterous. I couldn't believe he was relaying the story to me with a straight face. Not only that, but he had this dumbfounded look on his face as if he was actually telling the truth.

"Sebastian, you need to go."

"I know this looks bad and I know my story sounds even worse, but it's the truth. I put that on my son."

"Don't bring an innocent child into your foolishness. I would respect you more if you simply man up and admit you got caught out there. Now please leave." Sebastian stared at me not moving, which agitated me even more. "Now!" I hollered, before walking to the door and opening it.

"Kennedy, you're making a mistake."

"The only mistake I made was believing we could get back what we had."

Sebastian shook his head and walked out. I closed the door and although I wanted to cry, I wouldn't let myself. I felt I had already wasted enough tears on Sebastian.

Blair

"Did you read today's paper?" I asked Kennedy when she sat down at the table where we were meeting for breakfast.

"No, I haven't gone into the office yet. Why? What happened?"

"Cameron is the father of that woman's baby."

"What!" Kennedy said loudly, making everyone in the restaurant stare in our direction. She quickly lowered her voice before continuing. "I'm stunned. I mean, I know he knew there was a possibility the baby was his, but for some reason I felt that it would turn out he wasn't the father."

"Me too. I know this sounds crazy to say, but I'm glad that Diamond isn't awake to read about this. Of course, I want her to wake up, but hopefully the story would've died down by then. They have this on every blog; they were talking about it on the radio. It's like I know there has to be more important stories than this." I shrugged.

"You know when the media gets ahold of a juicy story they run with it."

"Yeah, especially when you a publicist feeding into the hoopla. Once again, this has Darcy Woods written all over it. I thought you were able to put a muzzle on her," I said, becoming annoyed.

"So did I, but you know the gloves came all the way off once Sebastian fired her. But I do think I need to have another conversation with Darcy. She needs a little reminder that I can still make trouble for her."

"When are you going because if I don't have Donovan, I will most definitely go with you. I would love to give Darcy's evil ass a piece of my mind."

"Don't worry, I'll handle Darcy. But speaking of Donovan, where is the handsome little fella?" Kennedy questioned.

"With Kirk. Last week, he asked me if he could come get Donovan for a few hours. Normally he visits him at my house, but he said he got his room all set up and he wanted Donovan to spend some time at his place."

"It's good they're getting some daddy/son time together, but I'm surprised he wanted to get him so early," Kennedy commented.

"That's crazy because I said the same thing. I was like why so early. He said he wanted to spend some time with him before practice. I was like whatever. Donovan gets up early anyway so why not. Plus, it gave me some free time to go see Diamond before I met you for breakfast."

"How was she... still no change?"

"Nope. Her mom was there. She's trying to be strong, but I can tell she's really scared. Cameron was coming in when I was leaving. I hope Ms. O'Toole don't try to knock him upside the head now that it's out he's the father of that woman's baby." I sighed.

"Are you joking or do you think she really would?" Kennedy asked, side eyeing me.

"Yeah, she would! I forgot you don't know Ms. O'Toole like I do. That woman don't play, especially when it come to Diamond and Destiny. The only reason she might not jump on Cameron at that hospital is out of respect for her daughter. She knows Diamond would never want her to do that. But I can't lie, I was tempted to smack the shit out of him myself when we crossed paths."

"I'm sure Cameron already feels bad enough. By no means am I defending him, but his wife is in a coma, his personal business about a baby he had outside of his marriage is blasted everywhere. Trust me, he is going through it."

"No doubt, but I don't feel sorry for him. The only people I'm worried about are Diamond, Destiny, and Ms. O'Toole. Diamond and her mother are so close. If Diamond doesn't make it, I don't know what she'll do. If the police hadn't killed Lela, I promise you Ms. O'Toole might've snatched her up for shooting her daughter."

"I still don't understand how a person can snap like that," Kennedy said, shaking her head.

"All because of Rico. Lela could never get over his death and she blamed Diamond. Now she's dead and Diamond is clinging on for life. Let's stop talking about this because I'm starting to lose my appetite."

"I feel you. We need to hurry up and order anyway because I'm sure you have to go get Donovan soon," Kennedy said, as she started looking through the menu.

"That's strange."

"What is it?" Kennedy asked, looking up.

"Kirk just sent me a text saying I didn't have to pick

up Donovan for a few more hours because he needed some more time."

"More time to do what?"

"I guess to spend with him, but I thought he had practice."

"Girl, who knows. I'm sure Donovan is having a good time with his daddy and that's all that matters."

"True that. I think I'll use the extra time to go get me a mani/pedi." I laughed.

"Now you're talking. And I think I'll have a couple of Mimosas to go with my breakfast. I prefer to be a little tipsy when I tell you what happened when I saw Sebastian."

"You saw Sebastian?! This I have to hear. Do tell," I said to Kennedy with a smile across my face, wanting to hear all the juicy details.

Diamond

"You so lowdown! I can't believe you have the audacity to show up here today after the world knows you had a baby with that Sharon woman," my mother yelled. When I heard the name Sharon it was like my ears perked up and my hearing became extra good.

"Ms. O'Toole, please don't do this right now. All I want to do is see Diamond," Cameron said.

"Diamond don't need to see you right now. Don't you have a newborn to tend to? Unless you plan on being one of those daddies that just send a check every month. Either way, it don't matter because you still trifling. My daughter don't deserve this and I don't want you no where near her."

"With all due respect Diamond is my wife. I have every right to be here and I want to spend some time with her before I go to practice. Now if you'll excuse me," I heard Cameron say. It was extra quiet and I didn't hear a response from my mother. The next sound I heard was the door closing.

"Good morning, baby. When I woke up, I couldn't

wait to come see you. You were on my mind all night, but that's nothing new because I think about you every second of the day. Baby, please, please, please wake up. I'm going through a lot right now and I need you by my side. I know I messed up, but I'm hoping when you wake up from this coma—because you will—that you don't leave me. Our marriage is the most important thing in my life so don't give up on us—on me," he pleaded and then it was like a spark had exploded through each finger, and up my arm, when Cameron placed his hand on top of mine. It was the first time I had felt any sort of physical sensation since being in my coma.

Dear God, is this a sign that I'm going to make it, that I'm going to finally wake up? God, please let me open my eyes so Cameron can know that I hear every word he is saying.

"Baby, I have to get ready to go. I wish I could stay longer. I love being next to you, but I need to get to practice. My game has been completely off since you've been in the hospital. But I keep trying to play because it's the only thing that is keeping me halfway sane. If I didn't have basketball to keep me busy I wouldn't be able to survive you being in here. I'll be back later on, I promise. I love you so much; don't ever doubt that.

Cameron, don't leave. There's so much I need for you to know. Just wait... I was thinking those words but once again, nothing was coming out. I heard the door close and a few minutes later I heard it open again.

"Baby girl, that husband of yours has got my blood boiling. I know I told you I would try and be respectful, but I can't do it no more. It's all in the papers that the baby is his. How dare he bring that sort of shame on his family? He don't deserve you. Diamond, you have to wake up so you can leave his dirty ass. You hear me! Do you hear me!" my mother kept saying over and over and over again.

"Yes, mother, I hear you," I said in a soft tone.

"Diamond! Diamond! Baby, did you just say something! Dear God, my baby is opening her eyes!" my mother screamed, putting her hands over her mouth.

"Mother, inside voice," I said, as her screams seemed to be amplified ten times louder.

"Keep your eyes open, baby! I'll be right back. I'm going to get the doctor!" she screamed again before kissing me all over my face and running out the door.

"Diamond, I'm so happy you're finally home where you belong," Cameron said, leaning down to kiss me on the forehead.

"You mean that? Even though I'm in a wheelchair and I can't walk?" I said, looking down at my legs. When I woke up from my coma, I soon realized that I couldn't feel anything from the waist down. The doctor was hopeful that within a few days that would change, but after a few weeks I still felt nothing and they decided to discharge me.

"That doesn't matter to me. I can hear your voice and wake up to your beautiful face. I prayed for that for so long and now it's come true."

"But I feel so helpless. I don't want you to have to take care of me," I stressed.

'That is what a husband is for. We took vows, remember, for better or for worse. I would do anything for you and you'll have all the help you need. All I want you to do is relax. Everything has already been set up in the house to accommodate you. There will also be a nurse aid coming in everyday."

"What about the therapist?" I questioned.

"I thought we could wait. Give you some time to get comfortable being back at home."

"I don't want to wait. I want to start getting therapy ASAP. I'm determined to walk again."

"Just give yourself some time, Diamond. There's no rush. Let me call your mother so she can bring Destiny home. I know she's anxious to see you."

"Why don't you go pick her up?"

"Are you sure you feel like making that ride?"

"No, you can go, I'll stay here."

"I'm not leaving you by yourself."

"I won't be by myself. Blair and Kennedy should be here any minute."

"Okay, but I'll wait for them to get here before I leave," Cameron said, then a few seconds later the doorbell rang.

"That must be them now," I said, moving forward as if to go let them in, before quickly realizing I was stuck in a wheelchair. I didn't know which one I was angrier about, being shot or being paralyzed.

"Diamond, you're home!" Blair and Kennedy beamed, as they greeted me with flowers, balloons, and a huge teddy bear.

"Yes, I'm so happy to see the two of you." I smiled. I needed my best friends more than anything right now.

"Baby, I'll be back. I'm going to get Destiny. Call me if you need for me to bring you anything home. I love you."

"I love you too," I said as Cameron walked out the door.

"You look great," Blair said, putting down the teddy bear and balloons next to me while Kennedy put the flowers in a vase.

'Thanks."

"Did Cameron pick out that dress for you?" Kennedy asked.

"Yep. He said he loves the way I look in pink."

"I agree. You're always so pretty in pink." Blair grinned.

"Then why do I feel so blue," I admitted, rolling myself in front of the huge glass window that overlooked Central Park.

"You've been through a lot. It's only natural you're not back to your normal self," Blair said.

"Will I ever be back to my normal self again? Can someone please define normal for me because that's the furthest thing I think I'll ever feel again."

"Diamond, you were in a coma and the doctor wasn't sure you would come out of that, but you did and you'll beat this too," Kennedy tried to reassure me.

"I pray to The Lord you're right. I can't see myself in a wheelchair for the rest of my life."

"And you won't be," Blair said, stroking my hair.

"I don't want Cameron to stay in a marriage with me because he pities me."

"Why would you even think that, Cameron loves you," Blair said.

"Blair is right. Cameron isn't with you out of pity, he is with you because he loves you," Kennedy added.

"A man has needs. And I'm sure his new baby mama

will be dying to satisfy them again." I laughed nervously.

"Diamond, don't let your mind start playing tricks on you. Cameron made a horrible mistake, but there is no doubt that he loves you and is committed to your marriage," Kennedy stated.

"I hope you're right because I don't feel like I can compete with a woman who has given my husband his first born son. If I stay in this wheelchair, I'll never be able to give him a child of our own," I cried as Blair and Kennedy held me tightly.

Kennedy

After I left my apartment the first stop I made before going into the office, was a visit to Darcy. I made sure to wear a bold, power red pantsuit that I had just got back from the tailor. I wanted Darcy to know that I meant business and I wasn't playing with her ass. My hair was slicked back in a tight ballerina bun. I had red lips with simple gold hoop earrings. I stepped off the elevator in my pointed black pumps with ankle straps, making swift and meaningful strides towards my destination. I felt as if I was on a conquer and destroy mission and I refused to lose.

As I got closer to Darcy's office, I noticed a shapely woman with bright sandy brown hair in Bantu knots prancing out with a huge smile on her face. Something about her seemed familiar to me for some reason, but I brushed it off as her probably being a party girl that attended many industry events. When we walked past each other she gave me a mischievous half smile that rubbed me the wrong way, but I was focused on my encounter with Darcy so once again I had to brush the woman off.

"Look what we have here. I see I arrived just in time," I said, walking in on Darcy and Sharon having an intense conversation. "Let me guess, the two of you are plotting your next tell all interview about Sharon's baby with Cameron. How long do you plan on stretching this story before your 15 minutes run out?" I stated sarcastically.

"My 15 minutes won't be running out anytime soon because the next story will be about how Cameron is leaving his wife for the mother of his son," Sharon shot back with way too much confidence for my liking.

Darcy gave Sharon an intense glare as if signaling her to zip it before turning her attention to me. "Kennedy, we must stop meeting like this. I never pop up at your office unannounced. I would really appreciate if you showed me the same courtesy," Darcy said politely. "With that being said, what can I help you with?"

"Help me? Is that a trick question, Darcy?"

"No. I know we've had our fair share of problems, but I'm hoping we can move past that. We're both successful businesswomen in a male-dominated industry, there's no reason why we should be enemies. We might never be friends, but we can surely be respectful to one another."

I was extremely suspicious of this new attitude Darcy was parading, but I decided to play along.

"If you genuinely want to help. Ease up on all these stories you have your client doing about her relationship with Cameron. Diamond just got out the hospital and as you can imagine she's going through a difficult time. Seeing your client splashed on everything discussing the child she shares with Diamond's husband is a bit much," I said being honest.

"Don't nobody care about what Diam—"

"What Sharon meant to say," Darcy interrupted, putting her hand up and cutting Sharon off mid-sentence, "is that we understand how troubling this entire situation must be for Diamond and we will ease up on the press."

Sharon put her hand on her hip and rolled her eyes at Darcy, obviously pissed about what she just said.

"Are you sure you're on the same page as your client?" I inquired.

"I'm positive. Aren't we on the same page, Sharon?" There was a long moment of silence as Darcy and Sharon stared each other down. Clearly Darcy won the standoff based on what Sharon said next.

"Yes, we are on the same page… for now." I heard Sharon mumble the last part under her breath.

"I hope I can count on you to keep your word, Darcy, especially under the circumstances. Like you said, we're both businesswomen. No need for things to get ugly."

"I agree. We've both done our share of mudslinging. I think it's time we took the gloves off and try to at the very least be civil to one another," Darcy said, extending her hand.

"Agreed," I said, shaking her hand before leaving. I left Darcy's office with even more questions than when I came. But my gut told me in time, all would be revealed.

Blair

"Thanks for meeting me for lunch," Skee said when I sat down across from him at Le Bernardin restaurant.

"Well, you know how much I love seafood and I heard they have the freshest and best in the city."

"So that's the only reason you decided to meet me?"

"That and it being on 51st Street between 6th and 7th Avenue, makes for a very short cab ride over," I teased. "But seriously I've missed you. We haven't seen each other since our Central Park stroll with Donovan."

"I know. I had a short overseas tour and you were the first person I wanted to see when I got back."

"That's sweet."

"It's true. You even wore your hair in my favorite updo style, with the bang slightly swooping over your eye."

"I never knew this was your favorite hairstyle," I said, feeling bashful all of a sudden.

"Really, you don't remember me asking you to wear it like that a few times."

"I figured you just thought it looked better with certain outfits I was wearing."

"You mean like the dress you have on now, where it's low cut and highlights your slender neck."

With only a few words and intense eye contact, Skee was slowly drawing me in, but I had no desire to go down that road again.

"I think we need to order our food," I said, trying to change the subject.

"Do you know what you're having?"

"Something light because in a few hours," I paused before looking at my watch, "I'm going to this dinner Cameron put together for Diamond at Jean Georges."

"That sounds nice. Will Kirk be there?"

"I seriously doubt it, but why would you even think that?"

"Things seem to be going well between the two of you."

"They're going okay."

"I assumed they were better than okay. I mean Kirk seems to be enjoying being a dad based off those photos he did for his upcoming *Sports Illustrated* feature."

"What are you talking about... what photos?"

"You haven't seen the outtakes *Sports Illustrated* released of Kirk and his son for the cover he's on? They've been all over social media the last couple days."

"I don't do social media," I snapped.

"I didn't mean to upset you. Why are you so angry? It's not like you didn't know they did a photo shoot together." Skee shrugged. "Wait, you didn't know?"

"Nope. He never told me a thing. I would never want Donovan's picture all over the internet and his face plastered all over a magazine. I can't believe Kirk would do something like that without discussing it with me."

"Wow, that's crazy. I wonder why he didn't say anything to you about it."

"Because he knew I wouldn't approve. He did that to get back at me."

"Get back at you for what?"

"You must have been out of town at the time but the *New York Post* ran a picture of us when we were walking in Central Park that time with Donovan. They ran a story you were the father of my child and Kirk was beyond furious."

"Yo." Kirk chuckled. "That's why when I hopped on Twitter for a brief second I was seeing all these congratulations in my timeline." He continued laughing. "I'm sorry, that's not funny. I mean for me, but not for you. That must've been hard on you."

"I didn't like it, but I wasn't having a meltdown over it either. I mean, the people that matter know who Donovan's father is but obviously Kirk needed the world to know. I never realized how huge his ego was until now."

"So you think it was about ego?"

"Of course. Even though the DNA results came back and he's the father I guess Kirk still sees you as some sort of competition. What he thinks you all is competing for I have no idea."

"You."

"Please. Kirk has moved on. He has a girlfriend," I said.

"Maybe, but I put my money on you still have his heart. And I hate to admit this, but I think he has your heart too."

"I won't deny that I do love Kirk, but as the saying goes that shipped has sailed. He was never able to forgive me for not being honest with him," I said, putting my head down.

"That's my fault and I should've said this a long time ago, but I'm sorry."

"Why are you sorry?"

"Because if I had let you move on and not drugged you that day, we would've never had sex and you would've been one hundred percent sure that Kirk was the father of your baby."

My mouth dropped as Skee said those words to me. Shock wasn't the correct term to describe how I was feeling.

"Initially, I thought you put something in my drink, but then when I asked you and you denied it I started thinking I was wrong. But I wasn't."

"No. Drugging you was the worse thing I've ever done to a woman in my life and I'll always regret it. I hope one day you can forgive me."

"Why... why would you do that?"

"I couldn't let you go. In my mind I felt you wanted to be with me too, but you were tired of my bullshit so you were fighting against it. I thought if I was able to get you back in my bed you would see that you belonged with me. I know it sounds fucked up, but I'm telling you the truth. And real talk, I still believed we belonged together up until a minute ago when I looked in your eyes and saw that you genuinely love Kirk."

"Skee, I'm at such a loss for words." My initial reaction was to reach over and slap him for all the trouble he caused but I held back because as outrageous as he actions were, the other part of me understood why Skee did it.

"I'm sure you are. I had no plans to ever tell you the truth, but I guess my conscious got the best of me."

"The crazy part is we did share something special, but on the flipside of that it was completely dysfunctional. The fact that you drugged me proves that very point. You're toxic for me and I don't think I'm any good for you either. But I do forgive you."

"You do?"

"Yes, because back then, a part of me didn't want to let you go. You had no right to drug me and it's beyond sick that you would do that, but I also know I was a different girl back then. I played my part in some of the things that were screwed up in our relationship. Now I'm a woman with a child and when you know better you do better."

"Damn, I love you," Skee said with all sincerity.

"I love you too, but I can't be with you." I grabbed my purse and walked out the restaurant without saying another word to Skee. At this point, I didn't even trust myself to have lunch with him. I wasn't completely over Skee and until I was, I had no intentions of taking any chances of falling back under his spell.

"Who is it?" I yelled out as I struggled to put on my other heel and zip up my skirt at the same time. I was rushing because I didn't want to be late for Diamond's dinner. "Who is it?" I called out again, still not getting a response only continuous knocking.

"I came to see my son," Kirk said as soon as I opened the door.

"Donovan isn't here and how many times do I have

to tell you to please call before coming over," I said about to shut the door.

"Where is he?" Kirk asked, placing his hand on the door so I couldn't close it.

"The babysitter is keeping Donovan at her place because she has another child she is watching too."

"So you're going out?"

"Yes, and I need to finish getting ready because I don't want to be late."

"Can you give me a few minutes because there is something I wanted to talk to you about?"

"Kirk, if it's about your upcoming feature in *Sports Illustrated*, I don't have time for it."

"So you heard?"

"Yes I heard, and if I wasn't in such a rush I would give you all the reasons why I'm so pissed at you, but like I said I have someplace to go. Now if you'll excuse me. I don't want to close the door in your face, but I will."

"Blair, don't do that. All I want is a few minutes. You can give me that," Kirk said.

I hesitated for a few seconds before giving in. "Fine, come in," I said, stepping to the side.

"I know I should've told you about having Donovan in the photo shoot."

"Kirk, you didn't tell me because you knew I would've never approved. I have no desire to have our son in the spotlight and I didn't think you did either."

"It was a one time thing. He's a baby. He won't even look the same in six months," Kirk joked. "But you're right. I knew you would say no that's why I didn't ask."

"Let me guess, this photo shoot went down that day you asked to get Donovan early in the morning. Claiming you wanted to take him to your house because you got his new bedroom all set up. I'm sure that was nothing but a lie."

"At the time it was a lie. But..."

"I knew it," I shook my head. "I need to finish getting ready. You said what you came to say and now you can go."

"I haven't said everything."

"What?" I snapped, ready to be done with this conversation.

"You have every right to be angry with me. I've been hard on you since I found out about the pregnancy and I'm sorry. I mean that, Blair," Kirk said, taking my hand. "I want things to be different between us."

"Thank you for the apology," I said, pulling my hand away.

"I can't touch you?" he asked.

"Kirk, like I said, I appreciate the apology, but when you say you want things to be different between us, I don't know what you want from me."

"I don't want there to be all this tension between us. I want things to be the way they used to be."

"You've really hurt me, probably more than anybody else ever has. Mainly because you were the last person I expected to be that cold to me."

"I was hurt too and I felt betrayed. For some reason Skee seems to really get under my skin. That's why I did that photo shoot. The thought of people thinking that anybody else was the father of that beautiful little boy other than me, and especially Skee, had me furious. It still doesn't make what I did right, but I wanted you to understand where my head was at."

"What about you bringing your girlfriend to the hospital on the day I gave birth to our son?"

"Blair, I'm so, so sorry for that. Again, my pride and ego had been hurt over you not knowing who the father of your child was. It was another way for me to strike back at you. But I promise I'll never hurt you like that again."

"I believe you."

"What about us?"

"What do you mean what about us, you have a girlfriend."

"I'm not even with her anymore and real talk it wasn't even serious. I never stopped having feelings for you, Blair."

"I never stopped having feelings for you either, but I'm not ready for this."

"Is there somebody else, maybe Skee?"

"No. It's over between me and Skee and there is nobody else in my life."

"Then what is it? Why can't we try to make this work? We share a son together, we should at least try for him."

"Kirk, I don't want you to be with me because of our son and I don't want to try and make things work with you just for the sake of our son. It's so much more complicated than that, but I'm running late. I really need to get to this dinner for Diamond."

"Okay, but promise you'll think about what I said."

"Of course."

"Thank you," Kirk said and kissed me on the cheek before leaving.

I never expected Kirk to come over and say those

things to me. I thought it was over for good between us and the idea there was still a chance to make it work and be a family, actually scared me more than anything. I didn't want to be hurt again and opening my heart back up to Kirk would make that a real possibility.

Diamond

"Having you all here... this is beautiful. Thank you for coming." I smiled. "I really needed this," I said, turning to Cameron.

"I'm glad you like it," Cameron said, softly kissing me on the lips.

"I'm going to like the food even better. You know French cuisine has become one of my favorites." I laughed nudging Cameron's arm.

"That's why I knew Jean Georges would be perfect.

"So sorry I'm late," Blair said, when the hostess brought her to our table. "I hope you got my text," Blair continued, giving me a hug before sitting down.

"Yes, I did. I'm just glad you made it."

"You know I wasn't going to miss your dinner. I heard of Jean Georges, but I had no idea it was located in the Trump International Hotel. Very nice and by the way you look beautiful tonight, Diamond."

"Thank you and so do you. I'm loving that fuchsia skirt."

"I'm so busy trying to get situated, I didn't even

speak to everybody. Excuse my rudeness. Hello! And look at Destiny over there looking so pretty just like her mother," Blair said, waving her hand. "Where's Kennedy? I know Miss Promptness isn't late.

"No, she went to the bathroom right before you walked in. I should've gone with her because I need to go."

"Baby, I'll take you," Cameron said, starting to get up.

"I can take myself. This power wheelchair can practically drive on its own. I'll be fine."

"Well, wait for me because I have to go to the bathroom myself."

"Come on, but you better keep up, Blair." I giggled.

"It's so good to see you laughing. You seem to be in a much better place," Blair said while we headed to the restroom.

"I am. Things have been a little difficult, but Cameron is really trying hard so it makes me try hard too. Going to physical therapy has been helping a lot also."

"That's wonderful, Diamond. I really do believe you'll be able to walk again."

"I know I will," I said with absolute certainty.

"I always loved and admired the fighter in you."

"You know how we roll!" I said, slapping Blair's hand.

"Wait... wait, what's all this hand slapping and stuff going on?" Kennedy grinned, coming out the restroom.

"Girl talk, but we'll fill you in after we go to the bathroom," I said needing to go.

"Cool, I'll be out here waiting for you guys," Kennedy let us know.

By the time I finished using the bathroom and got myself together, Blair was waiting outside the restroom talking with Kennedy. Their conversation seemed serious.

"Ladies, this is supposed to be a fun dinner, why so tense?"

"Tense isn't exactly the right word. I was telling Blair that I thought it was time she gets back to work. I've been getting a lot of phone calls and I thought she should take advantage of it."

"Yes, and you know Kennedy is all business all the time. I was explaining to her that I am ready to get back to work, but it has to be the right projects. I mean I'm a mother now so I have to juggle both."

"Blair, we're all aware you're a mother and that's a beautiful thing. Donovan is precious, but there are a lot of mothers that juggle both and so can you," Kennedy said in a sweet yet condescending way.

"Like I was saying to you, I get it," Blair barked back.

"Ladies, calm down. I'll say it again; this is supposed to be a fun evening. We can talk work tomorrow."

"Agreed, but I'm going to say this one last thing then I'm done," Kennedy said.

"Make it quick," I warned.

"Blair, I really love how you're embracing mother-hood and I see so many positive changes in you because of it. If you were working in any other industry I would tell you to take all the time you need. But this is the entertainment industry and we both know how this game works. There is a small window of time for you to really be able to shine and I just want you to be able to take advantage of it, but only if this is the career you truly want. Whatever you decide, I love you."

"Point taken," Blair said, hugging Kennedy. "I love you too."

"I love you both. That was so sweet, it makes me a little teary-eyed. Now let's go eat. I'm sure everybody is wondering where the hell we are." We all laughed as we headed back to the table.

"Diamond, who is that woman talking to Cameron?" Kennedy questioned, as we got closer to our table.

"I have no idea. I've never seen her before. Maybe she's just a fan."

"You mean groupie," Blair chimed in.

"I don't think she's either and we're going to find out," Kennedy said in a stern voice.

By the time we got to the table, the mystery woman was saying bye to Cameron and quickly walked off. But not before me, Blair, and Kennedy stared her down. We were looking so hard we could probably tell you the size and color panties she had on.

"Cameron, who was that woman you were talking to?" I asked.

"I don't even know her name," he said.

"Where do you know her from?"

"Just around," Cameron said. It was obvious to me from his body language that he didn't want to tell me.

"Can you please tell me where you know her from? Is she somebody you slept with?" I pressed.

"Diamond, no, it's nothing like that."

"Then just tell me!"

"She works at the place where Sharon and I had the DNA test. I didn't want to bring up Sharon and the baby in front of everybody while we're having this dinner for you," Cameron explained.

"It's fine," I said, looking over at Kennedy who seemed to be in deep thought after hearing what Cameron said. "Okay everybody enough of this small talk. Let's eat!" I cheered, clapping my hands and wanting this to be the beautiful evening Cameron had planned.

"Miss Lopez, can you get the door," I yelled out from the kitchen. A few seconds passed and the doorbell rang again. "Damn, I forgot Miss Lopez had a doctor's appointment this morning. She won't be in until later," I mumbled out loud on my way to get the door. "Coming," I yelled.

When I first opened the door I didn't say a word. I simply glared at the woman standing in front of me. I couldn't believe the audacity of this chick.

"Aren't you going to invite me in? Guess not so I'll just let myself in," the woman said, bombarding herself past me.

"Sharon, what do you want? Why are you here?"

"To see you. Why else would I be here," Sharon said with a nasty attitude. "So this is how rich people live," Sharon said with a wicked laugh as she looked around our penthouse. "Cameron has us living in a nice apartment, but nothing like this."

"Maybe because I'm his wife and you were a mistake."

"I'm the mother of Cameron's son and I'm no mistake. Me and my son deserve all the perks of being an NBA wife and we'll have it," Sharon shouted.

"Well when you do become an NBA wife, hopefully

it will work out for you and you'll receive all those so-called perks you desperately want, but until then get the hell outta my house."

"Before Cameron met you, we were very happy together. Things were good and they will be again. So don't get used to living here because this won't be your house for long, sweetie. Cameron and I will be a family and I'll be living here together with our son. It would already be happening if you weren't stuck in that chair. The only reason he hasn't left you already is because he pities your pathetic ass."

"Get out! Get out now!" I screamed. But Sharon didn't move. She stood over me like there was nothing I could do and for the first time in my life I felt helpless. I was thinking about all the physical therapy I had been doing for the last couple of months and how strong I felt while doing it. I was using that energy to almost will myself out of this wheelchair, so I could smack the shit out of Sharon before tossing her ass from my home.

"What are you going to do, Diamond?" Sharon mocked. "Nobody is here to save you," she said, walking to the front door and locking it. "It's just you and me."

"I don't know what you're trying to accomplish, but you're making a huge mistake. As a matter of fact I think I'm going to call Cameron right now and let him know that his erratic baby mama is here harassing me," I said going towards my phone.

"Don't you dare!"

"Or better yet, let me call the police. Maybe an arrest record will knock some sense into you."

"You won't be calling anybody!" Sharon roared, knocking the phone out of my hand. "I came here to get you out of Cameron's life once and for all so we can be a family and that's what I'm gonna do."

Maybe I'm slow, but it wasn't until this exact moment did I realize that Sharon was batshit crazy. When she first showed up at my door, I assumed Sharon was a bitter baby mama trying to cause drama in my marriage, but this was much worse. This woman wanted the same fate for me that Lela did—dead—and if I didn't think fast, she might get her wish.

Kennedy

"Kennedy, where are we going?" Blair asked as I almost had her running down Lexington Avenue to keep up with me.

"I will tell you everything when my suspicions are confirmed. Just keep up, we're almost there," I said, anxious to get to our destination.

It wasn't necessary for me to drag Blair with me on my mission, but I wanted a witness. Plus, if I needed to do some damage, I thought having Blair as backup would help. She did know how to turn up if necessary.

"We're here," I huffed, standing in front of the building.

"Thank goodness! I felt like you had me on a workout as fast as we were walking... I mean running." Blair sighed. "Now will you tell me what we're doing here?" Blair asked when we got in the elevator.

"Just follow my lead," I directed Blair right before stepping off the elevator. "There she is." I smiled when I saw the woman sitting at the receptionist desk.

"That woman looks very familiar. Isn't she—"

"Shhh." I wanted to hush Blair up since we were so close to the woman. She was on the phone and I wanted to catch her off guard. After the woman's call was over and she looked up, her mouth dropped.

"Can I help you with something?" the woman finally asked, trying to pull herself together and be professional.

"Hi Sonya. I'm Kennedy and this is Blair, but you already know that."

"Excuse me. I don't know you. What are you talking about?"

"Oh, but you do. You're the one that sent me the naked picture of Sebastian from his phone," I said, snatching her arm. "Blair, doesn't this tattoo look familiar to you?"

"Sure does."

"Get your hand off of me!" Sonya snapped, yanking her arm away.

"Isn't she also the woman we saw talking to Cameron at the restaurant?" Blair questioned.

"Yes, she is. What are the chances that the same woman that sent me the naked photo also works at the office where Cameron had his DNA test? But wait it gets even better. Sonya also knows Darcy."

"Darcy?" Blair repeated with a frown.

"That's right. I saw Sonya here prancing out of Darcy's office with a huge smile on her face several weeks ago. I don't think any of this is a coincidence at all. What do you think, Blair?"

"I have to agree with you. I think Sonya has been up to no good."

"Yep. Sonya, I'm going to need to see your boss immediately. He needs to know his receptionist has been up to no good," I said, ready to take her down for all the havoc she had caused.

"Wait! I'll tell you everything you want to know, but please don't tell my boss," she pleaded.

"She cracked sooner than I thought she would," I mouthed to Blair who then winked her eye on the sly.

"I don't understand why Diamond isn't answering her phone," I said to Blair as we headed out the office building.

"I know. Maybe she's in physical therapy and doesn't have her cell on her."

"Maybe, but let's stop by her place before going to see Darcy."

"Sounds like a plan because Diamond definitely needs to know what is going on.

Knock... Knock... Knock...

"She must not be here," Blair said after I knocked one more time and no one answered. "Let's go. We'll come back after we go pay a visit to Darcy.

"Okay," I said reluctantly. I felt uneasy about leaving. Blair was almost halfway down the hallway, but I was still standing by the door.

"Kennedy, why are you still standing there? Nobody is home. We'll keep trying Diamond on her phone. I'm sure she'll answer her phone or be back home soon," Blair said.

I put my finger to my lips, motioning Blair to remain silent. "Wait for me, Blair, here I come." Instead I put my ear to the door. I could hear some sort of commotion going on inside of Diamond's place and I knew something was very wrong. I walked swiftly, but quietly to Blair.

"What's wrong?" Blair asked in a low voice when I got next to her.

"I think Diamond is in danger. I heard some commotion."

"Are you sure?"

"Yes! I'm positive," I said adamantly.

"You stay here and keep your ear to the door. I'm going downstairs to get security and have them call the police," Blair said, heading for the elevator.

I went back to the door and knocked again. This time I stepped to the side so no one could see me if they looked through the peephole. A few minutes later, I could hear someone come to the door, but they didn't open it.

"Someone help me!" I heard what sounded like Diamond yell out. "Sharon is in here and—" before Diamond could finish what she was saying I heard what sounded like glass breaking. I started banging on the door loudly. I couldn't believe Sharon was in there.

"Diamond, I've called the police and they're on the way!" I screamed, continuing to pound on the door. I was hoping that if Sharon knew help was on the way it would stop her from doing whatever she had planned. I kept banging and wouldn't stop.

A few minutes later I heard the elevator door open and it was Blair with two security guards. "The police should be here soon," Blair informed me when they got to the door.

"Good because Sharon is in there with Diamond."

"What!" Blair exclaimed.

"Ladies, excuse me," one of the security officers said, using a key to open the door, but the chain kept them out. "Move back, we're going to have to kick it open," the other security officer said.

Luckily both men seemed to be physically fit, so although it took several tries they finally managed to push open the door.

"Get out of here or I'll slit her throat!" Sharon threatened holding a knife to Diamond's neck.

"Ma'am, we need you to put that knife down and come with us right now," one of the security guards said. When Sharon didn't comply, I was waiting for one of them to pull out a gun and threaten to blow her brains out if she didn't do as they ask, but then I noticed neither of them had weapons.

"What sort of security is this?" I whispered to Blair.

"I don't know, but hopefully the police will get here soon. Diamond looks so vulnerable in her wheelchair. I'm scared for her," Blair said nervously.

"I'm scared for her too. I wish the police would hurry up."

"I'm only going to say this one more time. Everybody get out or she's dead," Sharon barked, pressing the tip of the knife against Diamond's skin.

I saw a tear roll down Diamond's cheek and my heart began racing. Then in a totally unexpected move, Diamond balled her fist and swung her fist with all her might, knocking Sharon in the face. It caused Sharon to lose her balance for a second, but she quickly regrouped. She lunged forward to stab Diamond in her back, but in what can only be described as a miracle, Diamond stood up from her wheelchair and ran towards us. Sharon started chasing Diamond, but the security men immediately tackled her to the floor.

"Thank God you all showed up when you did," Diamond cried, running into Blair's and my arms.

"It's okay, you're safe now," I said holding Diamond tightly. "Come and sit down."

When we sat on the sofa, Diamond continued crying for the next few minutes. I think more than anything she was in shock by what had happened. A few seconds later, the police arrived and arrested Sharon. While they were putting the handcuffs on her wrist she was talking crazy, as if we hadn't all witnessed her trying to kill Diamond.

"I'll be out tonight. Cameron will never let the mother of his child sit in jail," Sharon said to Diamond as she was being escorted out.

"Officers can you wait one minute, please? There is something Diamond needs to know before you take this trash to jail," I told the police officers.

The officers stopped in front of us and Diamond glanced up at me with tears still streaming down her face. She had a confused look on.

"Kennedy, what's going on?" Diamond asked, trying to stop herself from crying.

"Sharon, not only will Cameron not be bailing you out of jail, but you won't see another dime from him ever again," I said.

"What the hell are you talking about? I'll be getting child support for the next 18 years," Sharon shot back.

"In the state of New York you don't have to pay child support for a child that's not yours." All the color drained from Sharon's face when those words came out of my mouth.

"Kennedy, I don't understand. What are you talking about?" Diamond was now completely baffled.

"Sharon and Darcy came up with a sick plan to deceive not only Cameron, but the courts. They hired Sonya, the woman we saw at the restaurant talking to Cameron to tamper with the results of the paternity test. Sharon always knew that Cameron wasn't the father of her son."

"He could've been if he had never met you!" Sharon screamed at Diamond. "You ruined everything."

Diamond tried to stand up and stumbled back at first, but on her second try she stood firm and walked over to Sharon. "You almost ruined my marriage with your lies and you tried to take my life. I feel sorry for that baby of yours, but thank goodness you'll be out of our lives," Diamond said before smacking the shit out of Sharon.

Diamond, Blair, and I stood and watched as the police hauled Sharon out the door. We held each other tightly, thanking God that we had gotten through this nightmare together.

Blair

"This has been the craziest week ever," I said flopping down on the couch.

"Who are you telling? Girl, I think I had about six drinks when I finally made it home." Kennedy laughed.

"I'm sure you did, but you have to admit, we do make a pretty great team."

"Yes, we do. That's why I wanted to run something by you."

"What is it?"

"Of course after I found out that Darcy had Sonya drug Sebastian and it was all a set up, I called him begging for his forgiveness."

"Yes, yes, and after he made you feel like shit for not trusting him he took you back with open arms."

"Something like that." Kennedy giggled. "You know Sebastian had been trying to get me to relocate to LA for awhile and before all that went down I planned on doing it."

"You're moving to LA!" I smiled getting excited for Kennedy.

"Yes, in a few months after I take care of things here and find a suitable office space in LA. So I'll be bicoastal. We'll have an office in NYC and LA."

"You making power moves. I like it."

"Do you like it enough to come with?" Kennedy asked me. "Before you answer, how great it will be for you career. After out talk you said you were ready to dive in. This is your chance. Like you said we're a great team and with both of us in LA, we'll make magic happen. Think about—"

"I don't have to think about it," I said, cutting Kennedy off. "I'll go. I'll move to LA too."

"Are you sure?"

"I'm positive. I think the move will be great for me and Donovan."

"How do you think Kirk will take it?"

"I think when I explain everything to him, he'll understand and be cool with it. I mean he plays basketball, his career takes him all around the world. I'm sure he can handle coming to visit Donovan in LA and of course we'll still be coming back to New York."

"Blair, I'm so ecstatic you're coming with me! This is going to be amazing!" Kennedy beamed, jumping up to give me a hug.

"I'm ecstatic too! Everything is coming together for all of us. Diamond can walk again, you and Sebastian are together again, I'm going back to work and to top everything off, Darcy Woods is out of business," I said hi-fiving Kennedy.

"Wasn't that article I had my friend at the *Post* do on Darcy fabulous," Kennedy bragged.

"Yes and she deserved to be dragged in the paper.

Having that woman tamper with the DNA results so it would come back that Cameron was the father of that baby was low even for Darcy. She'll never get another job in this town again."

"Maybe her and Sonya can stand in the unemployment line together," Kennedy added.

"I'm just glad the truth came out when it did. That was good detective work, Kennedy. Now we can all move on with our lives. LA here we come!"

3 Months Later...

"Kennedy, how in the world did you pull this off? I can't believe we're lounging on this ridiculous yacht right now as we sail around Sardinia for a freakin' week!" I beamed.

"I made a promise that if Diamond came out of her coma we would do our girl's vacay on a fabulous yacht and I wasn't going to break that promise." Kennedy smiled.

"If you had we wouldn't have been mad because this was one promise I don't think too many people could've kept," Diamond chimed in.

"You still haven't said how you pulled this off. This yacht has a helicopter landing pad and everything," I said, holding my glass of champagne, staring out at the seven-deck vessel that was equipped with a saltwater pool, climbing wall, library, health spa and an outdoor theater.

"It's amazing what favors you can get from a billionaire business magnate when you can get their kids favorite musician to perform at their birthday party." Kennedy giggled.

"You've always been so resourceful, that's one of the benefits of having you as a business partner." Diamond winked.

"Yeah, and as a publicist. You always deliver the goods, Kennedy," I added.

"Why thank you ladies. I appreciate all the kudos! This trip has been a long time coming and I'm so happy we were able to make it happen."

"Me too. This past year has been so crazy for all of us, we definitely needed this vacay and nobody deserves it more than you, Diamond."

"Thanks, Blair, but we've each had our share of drama."

"True, but it all worked out in our favor. Diamond, you survived getting shot, that lunatic Sharon, and saving your marriage. Blair is joining me as I start my new chapter in LA with my fiancé. I still love saying that," Kennedy laughed. "I had resigned myself to being single for the rest of my life and now I'm marrying Sebastian."

"Yep, we have another wedding to plan and I can't be more exited." Diamond smiled.

"Me too, but there has been a slight change in plans for me."

"What sort of change in plans, Blair?" both Kennedy and Diamond asked simultaneously.

"I've decided to stay in New York."

"What... why?" Diamond questioned.

"I want to continue to work and pursue my acting career, but instead of doing it in LA I'm going to do it in New York so that Donovan can be close to his dad and…"

"And because you and Kirk are getting back together!" Diamond beamed, clearly getting excited.

"Calm down. We're not officially back together, but we have decided to start dating again."

"Dating? How does two people who have a child together and were once in an exclusive relationship, revert back to just dating?" Kennedy inquired.

"You're both aware of all the bullshit I've been through with Kirk during and after my pregnancy."

"Yes, I still see daggers when I think about him bringing that hussy to the hospital after you had just given birth. Buuuuut… in the last few months Kirk really has done a 180. He adores Donovan and I know he love yo' ass! His pride and ego was hurt which caused him to behave very immaturely, but that boy does love you. So it would warm my heart if you all worked it out and we started planning your wedding too." Diamond grinned.

"No need to get fitted for a bridesmaid dress just yet. I want us to take our time, that's why we're dating. I don't want Kirk to be with me because he doesn't like the idea of me taking Donovan and moving far away or because he doesn't want to see me with someone else. That's why I'm staying in New York, so he can see his son whenever he wants and they can build their own relationship, separate from me. We can then start with a clean slate and date to see if we truly want to be with each other for the right reasons. What's most important to me is that we're both great parents to Donovan and that we're friends. If marriage comes from that then great, if not then at least they'll be a mutual respect."

"Part of me wants to cry because I was so happy you were coming to LA with me, but I do think that's a great change of plans," Kennedy admitted.

"So do I," Diamond agreed.

"Plus, I can still work magic for your acting career whether you're in New York or LA. Doing what's best for you and Donovan should always be your number one priority and I think that is what's best. I can't lie, I'm going to miss not having one of my best friends in LA with me." Kennedy sighed.

"I know. I was looking forward to our girls take over LA adventure too, but we'll definitely be coming to visit a lot," I said, giving Kennedy a hug.

"Since we're sharing and caring, I have some news of my own that I want to tell my two best friends," Diamond said, making it a group hug.

"Do tell!" I said as our eyes widened, anticipating what Diamond had to say.

"Get ready for Donovan to have a playmate!"

"OMG, you're pregnant!" I screamed.

"Congratulations, Diamond! I'm so happy for you," Kennedy said, with her eyes watering up. "I know how much you wanted to start a family with Cameron. Now Destiny will have a little brother or sister," she gushed.

"Yes. After all we've been through, I think we'll get our happy ending. Our marriage has gotten so much stronger and when I wasn't even thinking about it, I finally get pregnant. Not only is the timing perfect, but it's truly a blessing."

"And you deserve all of your blessings. I know Cameron is ecstatic. He's going to be such a proud papa," I said hugging Diamond even tighter. "I'm going to be such a great auntie/godmother."

"Ummmm, how do you know that Diamond doesn't want to make me the godmother?" Kennedy said, playfully rolling her eyes.

"I already got that covered. The little one will have two godmothers. You all know I don't really do things the traditional way." Diamond giggled.

"Works for us," Kennedy and I said, hi-fiving each other.

"Who knew we would be celebrating so much and our vacation is just getting started. As we start closing this year out, I think the next will be even greater," Kennedy said.

"I agree. I'm so happy to have you ladies in my life. I don't think I would've gotten through this roller coaster ride called life without both of you. We each took different paths in life, but all found happiness and that's what you call true success," I said.

"Amen to that! None of this means anything if you don't have genuine happiness, that is the true measure of success and so far in our journey, it's damn sure been rocky getting here, but we made it," Diamond added.

"Ladies, let's make a toast," Kennedy said, reaching for the champagne and refilling my glass. "Now I get why you've only been drinking orange juice." She laughed, pouring some more in Diamond's glass. "Everybody raise your glasses. Ladies, we defied all obstacles and made our dreams come true. To even bigger and greater things to come, 'cause we some ballers!"

"We really are some baller bitches, aren't we ladies," Diamond beamed.

"To baller bitches!" we cheered in unison, looking out into the ocean as the sun set over the horizon.

The End...

A KING PRODUCTION

Bitch

The Story Of Precious Cummings

MOVIE EDITION

A Novel

JOY DEJA KING

Started From The Bottom

Coming from nothing and having nothing are two different things. Yeah, I came from nothing, but I was determined to have it all. And how couldn't I?

I exploded into this world when hood rich wasn't an afterthought, but the only thought. You turn on the television or go on social media and every nigga is iced out with an exotic whip, surrounded by a bitch in a G-string, bundles down to her ass, poppin' that booty. So, the chicks in videos were dropping it like it's hot for the rappers, singers and athletes, while the bitches around my way were dropping it for our own superstars. Dealing with a street nigga on a legendary drug kingpin status was like being Beyonce herself on Jigga Man's arm. A bitch like me was thirsty for that.

I'd been on some type of hustle since I was in pampers. I grew up in the grimiest Brooklyn projects. It was worse than being in prison because you knew there was something better out there; you just didn't know how to get it. You never saw green grass or flowers blooming. Instead of looking up to teachers, lawyers, or doctors, you worshipped the local drug dealers who hustled to survive and escape their existence. Even as a little girl, I knew I wanted more out of life. Somehow hustling was in my blood.

First, I hustled for my moms' attention because she was too busy turning tricks to pay me any mind. I never knew who my daddy was, so while my mom was fucking in her bedroom, I would wait outside the door with my legs crossed, holding my favorite teddy bear in one arm as I sucked my thumb. When the tricks would come out, I would look at them with puppy-dog eyes and ask, "Are you, my daddy?" The question would freak them out so badly they'd toss me a few dollars so I would shut the fuck up.

One day when I was five, my mother was looking for something in my drawers, she came across a bunch of fives and tens and some twenties. The total was five hundred and some change. Of course, she wanted to know where all the money came from. When I told her that the money came from her business clients (that's what my mom called them), she lit up. She tossed me up in the air and said, "Baby, you my good luck charm. I knew one day you'd make me some money."

On that rare occasion she showed me mad love. As young as I was, I equated my mother's newfound interest in me with love. From that moment on, I learned how to hustle for my moms' attention, by providing her with money.

Somehow, my moms' customers never messed with or tried to fondle me. I think it's because even as a little girl I had this darkness in my eyes, that said, "Don't fuck wit' me."

By the time I was fifteen with all the tricks my mom's pulled, we were still dead ass broke, living in the projects. She couldn't save a dime because with hooking comes drugging and my mom's stayed high. I guess that's all you can do to escape the nightmare of having all types of nasty, greasy fat motherfuckers pounding your back out every damn day. The characters that I saw coming in and out of our apartment were enough to make me want to sew up my pussy so nobody could get between my legs, but my mother would soon change all that.

One day, I was sitting at home watching a weekly vlog on YouTube from one of my favorite social media influencers. She was doing beauty maintenance and self-care. I was completely caught up that I almost didn't hear my mother's bedroom door open. I heard the floor squeak and immediately turned off the television. Without a word, I started giving the living room a lick and a promise. I emptied several full ashtrays, picked up the dirty glasses scattered about the

floor and wiped off the cocktail table.

Out of the corner of my eye, I watched my mother stare at me for a few minutes. She had the strangest look on her face. She was holding a bottle of whiskey in one hand and a cigarette in the other. My mother was only 33 but living a reckless life filled with drugs and heavy drinking had taken its toll. With unkept hair, poor hygiene, and a nasty disposition, most of the time I couldn't stand being around her. There was no trace of the once curvy beauty that every hood chick envied. Her once long, wavy hair was now thin and straggly. The one-time ghetto queen was just a bag of bones that you wouldn't even recognize unless you stared deeply into the green eyes she inherited from her father.

It was the middle of the afternoon, and she was just waking up, still wearing her dingy nightgown, blowing smoke in the air. She held on tightly to her cigarette, staring at me as if I was a reminder of what she used to be in her prime.

"Precious, you sure are growing up to be a pretty girl." I stayed silent and continued picking up clothes that were scattered on the floor and then started sweeping. "Didn't you hear what yo' mama said?"

"Yes, I heard you."

"Well, you betta say thank you."

"Thank you, ma."

"You welcome, baby."

My mother walked over to the couch and sat down with her legs spread open. She took one last long pull from her cigarette and put it out in the ash-tray. She then took a swig from the whiskey bottle. The alcohol was spilling down her chin.

"Baby, you know that your mother is getting up there in age. I can't put it down like I used to. So baby, I was thinking maybe you need to start helping me out a little more."

Her comment made me pause and frown up my face. "Help you out more how? I basically give you my whole paycheck."

"Like I said, yo' mama can't put it down like I used to."

That bullshit made me stop sweeping the floor and I stared directly in my mother's eyes.

"What does any of that have to do wit' me? I bare-ly go to school as it is because what was supposed to be a parttime job at the car detailing shop is more like fulltime. Damn near every cent I make, goes in your pocket to pay bills."

"Baby, that little job you got ain't bringing home no money. It's just enough to maintain. I'm talking about getting a real job."

I started sweeping the floor again wanting to ignore the foolishness coming out her mouth.

"Ma, I'm fifteen. It's only so many jobs I can get and so much money I can make. My boss not even supposed to give me all the hours she has me doing at the shop. That's why she pays me off the books."

"Precious, as pretty as you are you can be making

thousands of dollars."

"Doing what? What job you know is going to pay a fifteen-year-old high school student thousands of dollars?"

"The oldest profession in the book...sex."

"You said that as if you asking me to do something as innocent as baking cookies for a living. You done lost yo' damn mind. What you tryna be now—my pimp!"

"You betta watch yo' mouth, little girl. I'm yo' mama. Don't forget that."

"Don't you forget it! You must have if you asking me to sell my ass so I can take care of you."

"Not me—us. Shit, I took care of yo' ass for the last fifteen years. Breaking my back and wearing out my pussy to provide us with a good life."

"This is what you call a good life?" I twirled the wooden handle of the broom around the living room as I looked at the cluttered two-bedroom apartment. The hardwood floors were heavily scratched with a few roaches crawling near the entrance to the kitchen. Visible holes in the walls and decaying window frames with cracks in the glass. My mother stood up real defiant like and pointed her finger at me.

"You listen here, a lot of these children around this way don't even have a place to stay. It might not be much to yo' ungrateful ass but it's mine."

"That's a lie. You don't even own this raggedy-ass apartment." We stared each other down for a few moments because I wasn't budging. "Sorry to disappoint you, but I'm not following in your footsteps by selling my pussy to some low-down niggas for money," I made clear then shrugged my shoulders brushing the bullshit off.

"Well then you betta start looking for someplace to live, 'cause I can't support both of us."

"You tryna tell me you would put me out on the streets!"

"You ain't leaving me a choice, Precious. If you can't bring home some extra money, then I'll have to rent out your bedroom to pay the bills."

"Who gon' pay for that piece of shit of a room?"

"Listen, I ain't 'bout to sit up here and argue wit' you. Either you start bringing home some money or find another place to live. It's up to you. But if you don't give me a thousand dollars by the first of the month, I need you out by the second."

"How the fuck am I supposed to come up wit' a thousand dollars by the first of the month?"

"I told you. You betta start using what's between your legs." My trifling mother then cut her eyes at my vagina before her skeletal body disappeared into her dungeon of a bedroom. She was practically sentencing me to the homeless shelter. There was no way I could give her a thousand dollars a month unless I dropped out of high school and worked fulltime at the detail shop. But what made this so fucked up was this had nothing to do with the monthly bills because she had

subsidized housing and received plenty of other help from the government. My mother basically wanted me to pay for her out-of-control drug habit.

Because the street life had beaten my mother, she wanted to beat me over the head with bullshit. But I refused to let that happen. I would hustle up that money, but I would do it my way. I was going to pick and choose who was able to play between my legs. My job at the car detailing shop was the perfect place for me to start. Nothing but top-of-the-line hustlers parlayed through, and one of them would be mine.

P.O. Box 912
Collierville, TN 38027
❀❀❀❀❀❀❀❀❀❀❀❀❀

A KING PRODUCTION

www.joydejaking.com
www.twitter.com/joydejaking
❀❀❀❀❀❀❀❀❀❀❀❀❀

ORDER FORM			
Name:			
Address:			
City/State:			
Zip:			

QUANTITY	TITLES	PRICE	TOTAL
	Bitch	$17.99	
	Bitch Reloaded	$17.99	
	The Bitch Is Back	$17.99	
	Queen Bitch	$17.99	
	Last Bitch Standing	$17.99	
	Superstar	$17.99	
	Ride Wit' Me	$17.99	
	Ride Wit' Me Part 2	$17.99	
	Stackin' Paper	$17.99	
	Trife Life To Lavish	$17.99	
	Trife Life To Lavish II	$17.99	
	Stackin' Paper II	$17.99	
	Rich or Famous	$17.99	
	Rich or Famous Part 2	$17.99	
	Rich or Famous Part 3	$17.99	
	Bitch A New Beginning	$17.99	
	Mafia Princess Part 1	$17.99	
	Mafia Princess Part 2	$17.99	
	Mafia Princess Part 3	$17.99	
	Mafia Princess Part 4	$17.99	
	Mafia Princess Part 5	$17.99	
	Boss Bitch	$17.99	
	Baller Bitches Vol. 1	$17.99	
	Baller Bitches Vol. 2	$17.99	
	Baller Bitches Vol. 3	$17.99	
	Bad Bitch	$17.99	
	Still The Baddest Bitch	$17.99	
	Power	$17.99	
	Power Part 2	$17.99	
	Drake	$17.99	
	Drake Part 2	$17.99	
	Female Hustler	$17.99	
	Female Hustler Part 2	$17.99	

QUANTITY	TITLES	PRICE	TOTAL
	Female Hustler Part 3	$17.99	
	Female Hustler Part 4	$17.99	
	Female Hustler Part 5	$17.99	
	Female Hustler Part 6	$17.99	
	Princess Fever "Birthday Bash"	$6.00	
	Nico Carter The Men Of The Bitch Series	$17.99	
	Bitch The Beginning Of The End	$17.99	
	Supreme...Men Of The Bitch Series	$17.99	
	Bitch The Final Chapter	$17.99	
	Stackin' Paper III	$17.99	
	Men Of The Bitch Series And The Women Who Love Them	$17.99	
	Coke Like The 80s	$17.99	
	Baller Bitches The Reunion Vol. 4	$17.99	
	Stackin' Paper IV	$17.99	
	The Legacy	$17.99	
	Lovin' Thy Enemy	$17.99	
	Stackin' Paper V	$17.99	
	The Legacy Part 2	$17.99	
	Assassins - Episode 1	$12.99	
	Assassins - Episode 2	$12.99	
	Assassins - Episode 3	$12.99	
	Bitch Chronicles	$40.00	
	So Hood So Rich	$17.99	
	Stackin' Paper VI	$17.99	
	Female Hustler Part 7	$17.99	
	Toxic...	$12.99	
	Stackin' Paper VII	$17.99	
	Sugar Babies...	$12.99	
	Deadly Divorce...	$12.99	
	The Legacy Part 3	$17.99	
	BITCH The Story of Precious Cummings	$17.99	
	Mastermind...	$12.99	
	Stackin' Paper VIII	$17.99	
	Stackin' Paper Holiday	$12.99	
	Mastermind 2...	$12.99	

Shipping/Handling (Via Priority Mail) $9.85 1-3 Books, $18.40 4-10 Books. For 11 or more $24.75.
Total: $_____FORMS OF ACCEPTED PAYMENTS: Certified or government issued checks and
money Orders, all mail in orders take 5-7 Business days to be delivered